I0659712

"Sadie?"

She jumped at the unexpected intrusion of her thoughts. She glanced at him before tying Sinatra's halter to the post in the bathing area. "Yes?"

He wiped a smudge of dirt from her cheek. "You know I would never intentionally do anything to hurt Walt or you, right? I appreciate the kindness and support both of you have shown me."

She swallowed hard at the feel of his caress. This man did things to her nervous system she'd never experienced before. She looked into his eyes and searched for any deception lurking in the depths. Again, she was struck by the color. "Where did you convince Gramps to go today? Or is the destination a secret as well?"

He held his hands up in surrender. "He took me to a local place that makes wine. He wanted to pick up a bottle. His idea, not mine."

She turned away to wash Sinatra. Great. Gramps purchased alcohol he wasn't supposed to have. Again. She stopped scrubbing and admitted, "It's hard for me to trust. Especially when I feel I've been lied to."

A heavy sigh reverberated around the area. "I don't like deception either." He paused before he continued. "I don't belong here."

She turned and witnessed him rubbing the back of his neck in a nervous gesture. The question bouncing around in her brain for days emerged, "Were you shot because you were doing something illegal?"

Praise for N. Jade Gray

RAIDER OF HER HEART
won Third Place
in the author's local writing group's
Right Hook Contest.

Raider of
Her Heart

by

N. Jade Gray

This is a work of fiction. Names, characters, places, and incidents are either the product of the author's imagination or are used fictitiously, and any resemblance to actual persons living or dead, business establishments, events, or locales, is entirely coincidental.

Raider of Her Heart

COPYRIGHT © 2019 by N. Jade Gray

All rights reserved. No part of this book may be used or reproduced in any manner whatsoever without written permission of the author or The Wild Rose Press, Inc. except in the case of brief quotations embodied in critical articles or reviews.
Contact Information: info@thewildrosepress.com

Cover Art by *Debbie Taylor*

The Wild Rose Press, Inc.
PO Box 708
Adams Basin, NY 14410-0708
Visit us at www.thewildrosepress.com

Publishing History
First American Rose Edition, 2019
Print ISBN 978-1-5092-2543-9
Digital ISBN 978-1-5092-2544-6

Published in the United States of America

Dedication

This book is dedicated to
the usual suspects of family and friends
who've supported me through the years:
God, Nathan, Blake, Mason, Mom, Dad,
Ornery Siblings, Nancy, Margret, Theresa,
and NOC chicks.

Acknowledgements

Special thanks to Melissa,
for eyeballing my bare-bones story and advice,
to Margret,
my red-lining grammar police and Beta reader,
Theresa, the encourager and Beta reader,
and Fawn, Beta reader.

~

I would also like to thank my editor, Nicole D'Arienzo,
for her help and support.

Chapter One

Kansas, August 21, 1863

The humidity hung over the night like a descending cloud as Judson Stone raced across the dry terrain. A trail of sweat snaked down his temple as another trickled along the indention of his spine. The moonless night echoed heavily with the sound of cicadas composing their music. He hissed an urgent command to his horse and leaned over Storm's neck as his mount picked up speed. The horse's hooves reverberated the message too late. Lord, he didn't want to be too late.

He was tired. Weary beyond belief. The constant threats made to the Union forces from the bushwhackers and the war had drained him. Peace, that's all he wanted. Was a little serenity too much to ask for?

A few hours ago, he'd been ready to crawl into his bunk after he'd returned from a scouting mission. He'd barely unsaddled his horse when summoned by his commanding officer. Minutes later, he entered the commander's office to see Colonel Thomas Ewing pacing.

"Sir, you wanted to see me."

"Stone. I need you to go back out. We've received word Quantrill and his raiders have planned a raid on the City of Lawrence."

The threat wasn't an unfamiliar one. He had heard this one before, but the concern written on Ewing's face created a foreboding chill to race down his spine. His gut twisted with a knot of fear.

"Do we know when, sir?"

"No, dammit. That's what has me worried. I need you to go to Lawrence and warn Mayor Collamore of the looming threat."

He had received his orders a few hours ago, and he'd raced toward Lawrence since. His orders were simple. Arrive in the town before Quantrill and warn the mayor.

His stomach churned, and his chest tightened. He swallowed hard as he fought the tension eroding his self-control. Would he make it in time? Could he thwart the plans before they were carried out? He squinted into the night as he determined his location from the terrain he passed. He'd always made this trip in the daylight, and the night shadows played tricks with his eyes.

He reined in his mount and glanced about to get his bearings. He fumbled with his canteen with impatient fingers before he dragged the container to his lips. He took a long draw but choked as water rushed in. The tepid liquid didn't relieve the dryness taking up residency in his mouth. He swiped a hand across his lower lip and replaced the cap. He believed he was in the vicinity of Eudora. Just a little past the settlement of Hesper.

The problem he faced was he didn't know if he was ahead of Quantrill or behind. The question had started to rattle around in his brain when the distinct sound of horses approaching reached his ears. He swiveled in his saddle and eyed the dark shadows of the road he had traveled. Had someone spotted him? He jerked on the reins and urged Storm off the road into the nearby trees. He placed a reassuring hand along the horse's neck and eased himself out of his saddle. A crop of trees provided cover as he crouched low and waited. The cicadas heavy song ended on an abrupt note, as the low murmur of voices carried on the night air.

He rose, tiptoed to pick up his horse's reins, and led him deeper into the shadows of some nearby trees. He tied him off to a low branch and crept back toward the road to resume his crouched position. Minutes ticked by before he caught movement from the corner of his eye. Two men on horseback rounded the bend. At first glance it was obvious the men weren't Quantrill or his band of raiders. He needed to keep moving. He eased away from his hiding spot but froze as one of the men chuckled and said Lawrence was in for a surprise.

Under his breath, he uttered a curse. In one fluid movement, he untied his horse's reins and swung up into the saddle. He had wasted precious time. He dug his heels into Storm's sides with a soft nudge and weaved through the trees to distance himself from the two riders. They were scouts for Quantrill. But how far were they ahead of their leader?

A mere second later, the report of a rifle pierced the night. He jolted at the sound and braced himself for the impact. Pain tore through his right shoulder. He clutched at the injury and drew back his hand to find his fingers sticky with blood. Damn. Slumping low over his mount's neck, he murmured a couple of reassuring words in an attempt to calm his edgy companion.

Twigs snapped a few feet away. His end was

near…sooner than he'd planned. The peace he prayed for was almost upon him, but he hadn't meant to gain serenity in this manner. He twisted in his saddle and stiffened his spine, as he waited to face the enemy.

Two shadows on horseback emerged. "Mister, doesn't this just cap the climax?" The speaker spewed something from his lips, and a deep chuckle rumbled in his chest. "Ol' Earl and me wonderin' what brings ya to this neck of the woods?" Another stream of spit emerged. "Better make your story good."

The other rider shifted in his saddle and shot an uneasy peek at his companion. "Les?"

"Clam up. We've got a job to do. No time for ya girly insecurities."

Judson cleared his throat. "Les? Do you always shoot first and ask questions later?"

The other man squinted at him in displeasure before he leaned over and decorated his boot with tobacco juice. "Mister, last chance. Why ya here?"

He forced a smile. "Well, there's a lady…"

He cut him off. "Bullshit. Ya the law? A soldier? You're dressed like one. Spill. Where ya going?"

He didn't flinch as he stared into Les's steel gaze. He clenched his jaw, but didn't break his eye contact, even as the other man drew his pistol. He aimed the barrel at his chest.

"I'm assumin' ya were headed to warn the good ol' people of Lawrence." He leaned forward and growled, "Get off ya horse."

He hesitated a moment before he swung out of the saddle and dismounted, holding his injured arm steady. He stared at both men in defiance. "You won't get away with this."

Spittle flew from Les's lips as he laughed. "Mister, I think we will." He pointed toward his companion. "Ya know of anyone here to stop us?"

Earl shook his head.

"Mister, turn around."

He stood firm.

The sound of a pistol being cocked reverberated through the stillness of the night. "Move it."

He shuffled about in slow motion, closed his eyes, and sent a quick prayer to his Maker. A saddle creaked and interrupted his plea. He opened his eyes moments before pain ricocheted through his head as Les brought his pistol down hard on the back of his skull.

He crumbled to the ground as he lost consciousness. He had found the peace he needed at last.

Chapter Two

Lawrence, Kansas, August 15, 2019

Sadie Winters flipped her turn signal on as she entered the Lawrence Memorial Hospital complex. She controlled the panic gripping her as she followed the signs toward the emergency room. Twenty minutes ago, she'd received a disturbing call. The nurse stated her grandfather, Walt Winters, had arrived at the hospital and requested they phone her.

She shoved the truck into park, grasped the door handle, and gave the lever a firm yank. She teetered as she jumped down before she settled onto the ground. With a flick of her hand, she slammed the door. Please, oh please don't let the problem be his heart. Nearly running across the parking lot she slowed her pace as she waited for the automatic doors to slide open.

Calm. She needed to remain cool. She glanced about until she spotted the registration area. The sound of her boots echoed on the linoleum floor as she crossed the room. The waiting area was void of anyone expecting to be seen. She stopped in front of the desk and shifted. She wrestled down impatience as she balanced herself from one booted foot to the other waiting for the clerk to finish a phone call.

The clerk smiled as she replaced the receiver in its cradle. "Can I help you?"

She tried to smile, but the fear of her granddad seriously hurt prevented the action from making an appearance on her lips. She glanced at the lady's nametag. "Yes, May. Someone called me to let me know my grandfather Walt Winters is here. Can you tell me where I can find him?"

The clerk glanced at her computer screen. "He's in exam one." She pointed down the hall. "First room on your right."

She mumbled a polite thank you before she rushed down the corridor. As she approached the curtain, she paused a moment, closed her eyes, and took a deep soothing breath. Whatever had happened she would get through. She hauled the curtain back and stuttered to a stop.

Her grandpa lay propped up on the exam table, a well-endowed nurse bent over him fluffing his pillow. His gaze sparkled as he peeked down the middle-aged nurse's shirt, a lecherous grin on his wrinkled face.

She was going to kill him.

"Gramps?"

He jumped, guilt in his startled gaze as it met hers. "Sadie girl. Come in. Come in. Nurse Joyce made me comfortable."

"I can see that," she muttered. She approached the side of the bed and glanced at her grandpa's left foot propped up by several pillows. "Goodness, what have you done?" The fear riding shotgun since she had received the call from the hospital slipped away. She hadn't found him on his deathbed. And if she had to judge by the twinkle in his eye, he wasn't anywhere close. She touched his hand to reassure herself he was okay.

He chuckled and scratched his chin, "How did work go?"

She leaned in, poked her finger continuously into his chest, and spit out in rapid fire. "Quit. Trying. To. Change. The. Subject."

"Hey, that hurts. I'm not a young pup anymore, you know." He rubbed his chest with a tentative hand and gave her a sheepish glance. "I don't think ya are going to like how this happened."

She tilted her head and studied his flushed face. She couldn't believe it. He shifted as he contained his embarrassment. This story had to be good. An impatient sigh escaped as she crossed her arms across her chest. "Come on, Gramps, spill. What did you do?"

He waited until the nurse left the area before he peeked at her and cleared his throat. He lifted his hand and wiggled several fingers for her to come closer. If possible, his blush deepened. "Remember the young filly, Rita, I've had my eye on down at the senior center?" He waited for her to nod before he continued. "Well, I convinced her to go out." He stopped before he stated, "Promise you won't get mad."

Geez, did she want to know the story? If he relayed a kinky exploit tale, she'd end up more embarrassed than her grandpa. She took a moment before she waved her hand in a go-ahead motion.

"I made an attempt to impress her, show her how agile I am. You know that's a plus for a man my age."

A blush stirred on her cheeks. Dang it, she didn't want to talk about his sexual encounter. She wasn't ready for this confession. She stumbled on her words, "I'm fine if you don't want to tell me. I don't need to know."

"No, no, Sadie girl. Confession, I hear, is good for the soul." He snuggled down on the fluffed pillow and fiddled with the blanket hem.

Was he stalling? "Come on already. What happened?"

"Well, she invited me over to her place for drinks."

"Wait." She held up a hand to stop him. "Hold on a cotton-picking minute. Are we talking leaded or unleaded drinks here? Please don't tell me you had alcohol."

He shot a hesitant glance in her direction. "I know I told you I wasn't going to indulge after the tequila incident, but she had these delicious Jell-o shots...."

She gasped, "You didn't? You know you're not supposed to have alcohol. At all. Period." She inhaled a deep breath before her blood pressure skyrocketed. She relaxed her jaw before she chipped a tooth. "How many did you have?"

He shrugged and didn't answer at first. His gaze met hers and he mumbled, "I lost track."

She closed her eyes for a moment before she ran a hand through her short locks. A groan escaped as she leaned over and whispered, "You haven't gotten to the part of the story on how you broke your foot."

"Oh, but it's not. Broken. According to the x-rays. Doc said it's a bad sprain."

She counted to five before she replied, "Okay, I'm glad your foot is still intact, that's a bonus. Please, continue."

"Well, after who knows how many Jell-o shots we decided to jitterbug. My mom's favorite dance if you didn't know. We used to dance a lot when I was a young pup." He shook his head. "Have I already told you that?"

She gritted her teeth in frustration. "Gramps, I'm not a total idiot. I've seen you doing the jitterbug around the house when you thought I wasn't around."

"Yeah, well, I'm not sure how the accident happened, but I was kicking some serious jitterbug behiney when the next thing I knew I landed flat on my back and stared up at the ceiling."

She straightened and stared at her grandpa for a few moments before she realized she couldn't hold the laughter at bay. Her amusement started as a small guffle and grew. She took a moment to try to contain her merriment. The picture she'd drawn in her mind of her grandpa kicking hiney and downing jello shots was too much. She swiped at the tears as they streamed down her face.

After a few seconds, he joined her in laughter.

She sucked in a breath and shook her head trying to get her merriment under control. She placed her forehead against her grandpa's. "I only have one question. The fair Miss Rita, did she dig your moves?"

He smiled and winked. "Totally."

She shook her head again. For a sixty-eight year old man his activities always made her question who the grown up was in their household.

She tucked the blanket around his frame. "Has the doctor indicated when I can bust you out of here?"

Before he could answer, a commotion from the other side of the curtain shattered the quietness of the ER. She drew the partition back and peeked around to see the staff rush to the entrance as an ambulance arrived in the outside bay.

Seconds later a gurney wheeled through the sliding

doors as a man thrashed against the restraints strapped across his chest.

The patient yelled, "Let me go, damn it. Take these ropes off. I've got to get to Lawrence. You don't understand. Their lives are in danger." She could feel the raw panic in the man's deep voice from across the room.

As the ER team drew near, the man's desperate gaze locked on hers. She tried not to gasp at the unkempt man. Twigs and dirt clung to a scruffy beard that would've rivaled the Robertsons from Duck Dynasty. Thick curly black hair adorned his head and needed a good trim. Grime about two inches thick covered the rest of his features. A deep red stain had taken up residence on his dark blue shirt. A shiver crept down her spine as his haunted gaze conveyed to her a terror she couldn't comprehend.

She overheard the paramedic state the victim had a gunshot wound and lost a lot of blood. Shot. Backing away, she veered from the scene outside the exam room. She trembled as she brought her hand to her brow. What could have happened?

"What's the problem, Sadie girl?"

She turned and forced her unease away. "Someone has been brought in by ambulance. I believe we may be here awhile."

He rubbed his chin and replied as another blush colored his cheeks, "You got distracted by the activity outside in the hallway. The doc wants me to stay overnight."

"For a sprained ankle?"

"Well, I bumped my noggin' when I slipped and fell. I have a goose egg on the back of my head. Guess the doc wants to make sure I don't have a concussion or something else wrong."

She leaned over and gave him a kiss on his grisly cheek. "I think you jarred loose a few marbles. I'm glad the doctor is erring on the safe side." She picked up her purse and glanced at her watch. "I'll be back in the morning. I need to tend to the horses. Please, don't give the nurses a hard time. I can't pick you up in the middle of the night for bad behavior."

He indicated his foot. "What trouble could I get into?"

She shook her head. *What trouble indeed?* "I'll see you tomorrow."

****

The faces leaning over him blurred as Judson struggled to stay alert. Unfamiliar sounds and sights tripped his heart faster than a jackrabbit flushed out by a coon dog. He had awakened in some box big enough for himself and two others. When he had struggled to exit, they slapped leather bands across his chest and he had yet to figure a way out. What hell had Quantrill's men placed him in?

A woman's voice fought in his clamoring brain to be heard. "Sir, you've been shot. They are taking you into surgery to remove the bullet. Please, try to relax and the operation will be over soon."

He had to escape this rolling bed. Images from the war flashed in his brain as he remembered fellow soldiers missing limbs because some field surgeon hacked on them. He renewed his struggle against the binding that imprisoned him and begged, "No. Don't let the ol' sawbones near me."

He cringed as something sharp pinched his arm.

"What are you doing to me?" He fought to keep his eyes open. His fingers slipped as he tried one last tug to gain freedom before he lost consciousness.

Chapter Three

Judson jerked and clawed his way back to wakefulness. His eyelids were heavy. What unseen force held them down? He blinked and focused on his surroundings. Damn. A newborn kitten had more strength than he had at the moment.

He took a deep breath before he frowned in bewilderment. Could he be in Heaven? If so, the Promised Land sure smelled peculiar. The odor wasn't like the stench of death he had experienced in battle, but more of a pungent smell irritated his nose. His mind didn't want to cooperate.

He shook his head to clear the fog lurking in his brain. He'd had orders. What were they? His eyelids drooped as he fought to recall.

In a flash, his eyes flew open. He'd been shot. The sawbones. He'd been fighting the restraints before he'd lost consciousness. Did they remove his arm? Bile rose in his throat as his stomach churned. Dare he inspect the damage inflicted?

He hesitated a moment before he raised his left hand to his shoulder. A breathy laugh escaped his lips as he lifted his right arm and discovered a whole limb. The ol' sawbones had spared him.

Relief flooded through him. He leaned forward and groaned. His body protested at the movement. Every single joint was stiff. He hadn't ached this bad since his last bout busting bronc's.

A wave of unease quivered down his spine. The surroundings he found himself were strange.

The walls were a brilliant white. Made brighter by the blinding sunlight filtered through the strange slats covering a pane of glass. A couple of closed doors hung adjacent from where he lay. A faint beep brought his attention to a weird box by the bed on a shiny stick.

What the hell? Flashing numbers and lines bounced across the smooth surface.

"About time you woke up."

A voice full of gravel startled him. He peered at the older man in a bed a few feet from his own, a newspaper spread out on his lap.

"My name is Walt. Walt Winters. What is your name, son?"

He opened his mouth to reply when the other man continued before he had a chance.

"What's wrong? Cat got your tongue?"

He cleared his dry throat and croaked. "No, sir."

He shook his head and chuckled, "What happened to you? I know how I got my bump on my head. I bet the knock on your noggin' and the bullet in your body would be a far more interesting story."

He closed his eyes. Did he know what happened? He shook his head as he wondered about the events of the evening before. His gaze shifted back to the curious codger. Could he trust him? Should he ask about his strange surroundings and what happened? He leaned back in the bed and stiffened as a sharp pain blasted through his right shoulder. Would he hurt this much if he were dead or inside a dream?

"Want to read some of the newspaper? They have a

great spread on Lawrence, since the anniversary of Quantrill's raid occurs next week."

He jerked to attention. What did the old man know of the attack? He spoke as if the assault had already occurred. Did he miss his chance to warn the town? His fingers shook as he rubbed his face. A strange clear tube protruded from his hand. He studied the object a moment before he yanked at it. He needed to get out of here. He'd wasted who knows how much time.

A gasp from across the room had him pausing in his attempts to free himself. A lady dressed in a bright pink top and trousers that matched hurried across the room and grabbed his arm.

"Don't remove your IV." She fiddled around to make him comfortable before she gazed down at him, a smile on her face. "There, as good as new. The doctor should be in to check on you in a moment." She fluffed his pillow one last time and scurried away.

He closed his eyes and questioned his sanity. He'd failed on so many levels. What had the outcome been for Lawrence? Had they been warned of Quantrill's impending arrival? He shot a quick glimpse at the occupant in the other bed. The older man ignored him as he studied the paper spread out on his lap. He frowned. What was the man's name? He racked his brain a moment before he recollected. Dare he ask about the raid he'd mentioned? He cleared his throat. "Walt?" The old man's gaze settled on him. "Can you read to me about Lawrence?"

Chapter Four

Sadie smothered a yawn behind the back of her hand and leaned against the wall of the elevator. She hadn't slept well last night. She'd tossed and turned as her thoughts focused on all the chores she'd have to take over for Gramps while he recuperated.

An eerie silence greeted her as the doors swooshed open. No one sat behind the desk at the nearby station. She paused. Where were the nurses?

A burst of laughter filtered from room two hundred ten. She chuckled and shook her head. She had found the staff. Ten to one they were in Gramps' room.

She paused inside the door and leaned against the doorjamb. She smiled and tucked an errant curl behind her ear as she watched her grandfather illustrate part of his story with his hands. Two nurses stood near the edge of the bed and giggled at his antics. A breakfast tray lay in front of him, forgotten. As far as she could tell, he hadn't taken a single bite.

A chuckle bubbled in her chest until her gaze landed on the other occupant in the room. Her merriment died in an instant.

The shooting victim from the previous night sat propped up in the adjacent bed, his gaze upon her. The dirt and debris no longer coated his hair and beard. His eyes were a startling aquamarine, like the Caribbean waters. He held her gaze in rapt attention a moment before she broke the contact. The panic she'd witnessed from him the night before didn't seem to be in attendance.

She sidled into the room and ignored the other patient. "Gramps, don't you think you've monopolized these ladies long enough? Your breakfast has gotten cold."

"Sadie, girl. Good morning." He cast a guilty glance at the two young nurses. "Sorry, I didn't mean to bend your ears for so long."

The nurse closest to him patted his arm. "That's all right, Mr. Winters. We've enjoyed hearing your stories." Both smiled at him before they left the room.

She leaned over to study the now congealed scrambled eggs and slices of bacon on his tray. "I brought the newspaper if you want to read while you eat your wonderful cold breakfast."

He waved her offer aside. "I've already read the paper." He shoveled a bite of egg into his mouth and grimaced.

She chuckled. "Now do you regret flapping your gums as long as you did?"

Judson shifted in the bed and stared at the partial barrier hiding the other occupants in the room. The old codger could weave a good yarn. He'd been as mystified as the nurses.

He shook his head as his earlier conversation replayed in his mind. The old man had to be senile. Disbelief still stiffened his spine. The news story he'd read to him couldn't be true. How could it be?

He'd been on his way last night to check the reports of an impending raid by Quantrill. Last night. Not over one hundred and fifty years ago. What utter nonsense.

All the destruction and the lives lost fell on his shoulders. He rubbed a shaking hand down his face. Could what the old man read to him be true? He couldn't accept his claims. His gut bunched as his stomach twisted in a knot. He'd blown his mission. Could he have done something different to prevent the horror? Frustration and panic made his head throb.

He shut his eyes. What limbo did he find himself? Had he escaped one hell to be placed in another? The endless questions plaguing him had no reasonable answers.

Above the whispers from the other part of the room, his stomach protested in hunger. When had he eaten last? He struggled to uncover the breakfast tray in front of him. He grimaced. If he was indeed in the future, the rations didn't appear to have improved over the years. He picked up the fork resting by the plate and poked a tine at the rubbery eggs. Indeed, he found himself in Purgatory.

He gave a tentative sniff before he took a bite. Surprise spread across his taste buds. The meal tasted better than it seemed. He'd managed to devour most of the meal before he swallowed wrong. He gasped and choked, knocking over the coffee cup in front of him.

The curtain dividing the room wrenched aside as the young lady he'd studied earlier rushed to his side.

"Are you all right?" She eased him forward, patted his back and offered him a drink with her other hand.

He leaned in and took a sip. The cool liquid soothed his throat.

"Better now?" The concern on the woman's face still had him struggling to breathe normal. Her vivid blue eyes peered at him in worried concern.

He nodded and studied the woman. "Are you an angel?" Had he voiced the question aloud? Her appearance wasn't what he expected, if she was indeed an angel. Her short black locks were as dark as midnight and lay softly on her head. He studied her sheared hair. Had she been ill?

"An angel?" Confusion clouded her question. "No. Why would you ask me that?"

He frowned and refrained from answering.

She tilted her head and studied him a moment before she asked, "Are you sure you're okay? You seem pale. I could call the nurse."

He shook his head. "Nay, I'm fine." His voice sounded like an unused rusty gate.

"Have you finished your breakfast? I can move the tray out of the way if you would like."

He'd lost his appetite anyway. He indicated she could remove the dishes. She turned and placed the tray on the counter behind her.

She glanced in the mirror hanging on the wall and considered the reflection of the man in the bed. His sharp gaze connected with hers. He had to be wearing colored contacts. A warm flush climbed into her cheeks at his unflinching scrutiny.

She turned and approached the bed. "Your bed is at a crazy angle. Aren't you uncomfortable? I can see why you choked. Anyone would in that position." She picked up the remote. "Is your button not working?" As she pressed the arrow, the bed adjusted. The man's spine stiffened and his knuckles became white as he clenched his hands.

She gasped and dropped the remote as he grabbed

her wrist.

"Where in the hell am I?"

She stumbled back a step and yanked her hand from his grasp. He had to be insane "I'm sorry. I only wanted to help." He glanced away, but not before she'd glimpsed the haunted expression reflected in his gorgeous gaze.

His hand shook as he scratched his beard. He speared her gaze with his own. A pained expression crossed his face. "Ma'am, I'm sorry. I didn't mean any harm. You startled me."

Her hand fluttered to her side. "I didn't mean to frighten you. I'll leave you alone so you can get some rest."

"Wait." He paused as his gaze darted toward the entrance to the room. "Am I in Heaven? Or am I in Hell?"

She shook her head. Disbelief rattled around in her mind. Did her ears deceive her? Why did he think he was dead? Who had scrambled his brains? "You're at Lawrence Memorial Hospital."

He froze. "I'm in Lawrence?"

She studied the man and the confusion radiating from his body. "Yes."

He frowned and leaned forward. "I need to warn Mayor Collamore. The town is in danger. Can you get me out of here and take me to him?"

His angst crackled between them. She frowned and took a step back, not understanding his desperation. Collarmore wasn't the name of the current Mayor.

His voice cracked as he pleaded. "Please."

"Excuse me."

She squealed in alarm. Her hand flew to her chest

as she spun. A police officer lurked just inside the room's partition.

"Sorry, ma'am. I didn't mean to frighten you. I need to ask the patient some questions about the shooting."

She stepped aside. "Oh, of course. I'll get out of the way." She cast a sideways glance back at the man in the bed before she stepped to her granddad's side. "Gramps? When will the doctor release you?"

"Shhh."

"Gramps," she whispered in disapproval.

"Dag nab it. Shh." He pointed to the curtain. "I want to hear the conversation."

He placed a finger to his lips and frowned.

She crossed her arms across her chest, eased down to sit in the nearby chair and waited in silence. In the back of her mind she wished to know as well.

Judson eyed the tall man before him in the strange uniform. He needed answers. Something he wasn't sure he could provide.

"Good morning. I'm police officer Brody Williams. I've got a few gaps I need your help filling in. The paramedics were sketchy on the details. If we're going to catch the person responsible, I need you to tell me what happened." The officer patted his front pocket and extracted some paper. "First. Can I get your name?"

He cleared his throat. "Judson Levi Stone."

"How old are you?"

He fingered the blanket covering his legs. "I turned twenty-nine my last birthday."

"Can you tell me where you're from?"

He hesitated. How much personal information

should he share? "Kansas."

The officer raised a brow at his vague answer before he shook his head. "Your occupation?"

He frowned. "My occupation?"

The officer sighed. "What do you do for a living?"

He rubbed a hand through his beard. He recalled his earlier conversation with the old man. What should he say? If he lied and they found out, what would the consequences be? He felt he needed to tell the truth in this situation. "I'm a scout with the Eleventh Kansas Infantry. I mean Cavalry. The name recently changed."

The man paused in scribbling on the tablet he held and gave him a stare he couldn't decipher. "Okay, I'll play along. Just for grins why don't you tell me your commanding officer's name."

"General Thomas Ewing, sir."

A resounding click sounded from the man's writing utensil. "I suppose you'll tell me next Quantrill shot you?" Sarcasm dripped from the question. "Listen, I'm here to help you and I can't if you aren't honest. We need to find the responsible party who shot you. So, if you could dispense with the baloney I would appreciate it."

A kernel of anger unfurled in his stomach. He'd told the truth, dammit. The man standing in front of him had ridiculed his answers. Had everyone lost their ever-loving damn minds? He ran a hand through his long locks. What in hell was going on?

"Judson? Did you see who shot you?"

Not meeting the officer's gaze, he took a deep calming breath. Should he give an honest answer? Would his response be met with the same distrust earlier displayed? "There wasn't a moon last night. I couldn't see the man's features." Why didn't he give a detailed description of Les? Or Earl?

"All right. Can you tell me the events leading up to when you were shot?"

He closed his eyes, shook his head and leaned back against his pillow. "Everything is a blur. I'm not sure." The lie left a bitter taste in his mouth. He opened his eyes and met the officer's gaze.

The man in uniform studied him a moment before he flipped his tablet closed and placed it back in his pocket with his writing utensil. "I'll leave you to get some rest." He produced a card and placed it on the table by the bed. "Give me a call if you should remember any useful information. My number can be found on the card."

Chapter Five

"Thank you, Dr. Adams. I will see Gramps follows your directions to a T." Sadie took the discharge papers from the doctor's outstretched hand and placed them inside her purse. This hospital visit couldn't end soon enough. The other occupant in the room had left her unsettled earlier.

"Now, for Mr. Stone's orders."

She glanced up from retrieving the keys from her purse. "Excuse me? What?"

Gramps cleared his throat. "Uh, Sadie girl. About that. I hadn't gotten the chance to tell you. I've asked Judson to come stay at the farm while he heals."

Shock rippled along her spine. Words were impossible as she stared at the sheepish expression upon her grandfather's face. He pulled fast ones on her daily, but this took the cake. His suggestion was preposterous. The man sharing this room arrived at the hospital shot, for mercy's sake. Did she want someone who could be a criminal at the farm?

He continued his conversation, not giving her a chance to respond. "I've already talked the proposition over with Officer Williams. He knows where Judson will be."

Her heart skidded to a stop a second before it began pounding in an erratic fashion. He'd already cleared this adventure. But not with her? A wave of

25

hurt threaded through her body before anger took its place. She gritted her teeth to keep from saying what she wanted to say. *One, two, three...* The mental countdown helped, but she took a calming breath as well. She focused her attention back on the doctor who appeared amused at the exchange.

"Well, I guess Walt wants to play nurse maid. What instructions does he need to follow?"

Her ire was wasted on the doctor as he gave her a kind smile. "I've prescribed an antibiotic and some pain medication for Mr. Stone. Walt says he uses the pharmacy on 6th Street. We've called in the prescription at that location." He glanced sideways at Walt. "The wound will need to be kept clean and dry. Give me a call if redness or concern of infection occurs. I've set up an appointment for Judson to see me in a week's time."

She wanted to smack Gramps as the doctor held the instructions out to him and he waved them off. "Sadie girl, can you handle the paperwork? I'll lose 'em."

She imagined herself giving him a whack to the back of his head before she took the papers from the doctor. "The instructions sound easy enough, even a chimp should be able to handle them." She caught her grandfather's gaze, but as if by magic he'd found a piece of lint on his jeans needing his attention.

The other occupant in the room had sat silent in a wheelchair a few feet away while they had discussed his care. His shoulders slumped in noticeable relief. Had he been worried she would say no? Did he not have anywhere to go? She forced a smile to her lips. "Well, I guess I need to introduce myself. My name is Sadie Winters. I'm this old softy's granddaughter." She extended her hand. He hesitated a second or two before he took it into his for a firm shake.

"Judson Stone, ma'am. Glad to make your acquaintance."

An unfamiliar awareness, sharp and quick slid from the tip of her pinky to the pit of her stomach from both the touch and his deep baritone voice. She dropped his hand. "I'll get the truck and park outside the front doors. The nurses will wheel you down to the entrance. I'll leave you both in the staff's capable hands."

A pent-up groan emerged once she exited into the hallway and stood in front of the elevator. She needed to have her head examined. Why had she let him talk her into taking a stranger home?

Judson shook his head as she retreated from the room. Her blue eyes had flashed fire before she exited. She'd been annoyed. A light fragrance lingered in the air along with the faint smell of horses.

A wave of elation surged through his system. He'd been scared. Scared. Him. He'd been a little unsure of how the old man handled the situation, but relief coursed through his veins at the outcome. "Walt, I think you should have asked her first if I could stay at your home."

He sighed. "I know I was a little high handed, but it's better to ask forgiveness. Trust me. Besides, I didn't want to give her the chance to say no."

He couldn't understand his insistence on helping him. "Why?"

"Son. Can I ask you a question?" He waited until he nodded his consent. "Now, be honest. Did you tell the police officer the truth when you told him you are a part of the Eleventh Kansas Cavalry?"

The question made it obvious the old codger had listened in on his conversation earlier. He gazed into the sun-weathered face and debated on whether to trust him or not. He swallowed and nodded. "Yes, sir."

"You're not part of a reenactment group for the anniversary of the raid, are you?"

"No, sir."

He nodded and replied, "You've had a shock, a knock on the head and shot. But I think you believe what you said to be true. I hate to be the bearer of more bad news, but the Eleventh Kansas Cavalry disbanded in Eighteen Sixty-five. We live in the year Twenty Nineteen."

His snort of disbelief cut short at the seriousness in the older man's gaze. He closed his eyes. First, he'd been read the newspaper story about Quantrill's raid over one hundred fifty years ago, and now…he spouted more nonsense. He had to be either senile or crazy. Could he believe such outlandish tales? He swallowed as a deep fear filled his mind. If he understood the words of the other man, he'd travelled into the future. Maybe he suffered from insanity. "You're trying to tell me I'm in the future? How?" He ran a hand through his hair. "What happened to me?"

Walt guided his wheelchair closer and patted his hand. "Don't fret."

"You think I need to be committed, don't you?" He squinted at him. "Why did you offer your home if you think I'm crazy?"

"Now, lad, I didn't say I thought you were insane. There's an explanation, and I will help you figure out the answers."

He remained quiet as two nurses entered the room.

One dressed in bright pink and the other in blue. "Are we ready to go, gentlemen?"

"Ladies? Can we have a race in these contraptions to the elevator?" Gramps winked at him.

The nurse in pink giggled and rapped him on the arm. "Oh, Mr. Winters, you'll be missed around here."

His brain scrambled with a ton of questions as the nurse wheeled him from the room. He found the surroundings outside of the room just as foreign. He tuned out the other noises around him as he pondered how he'd lost over one hundred fifty years in a blink of an eye. How in the hell had it happened?

Chapter Six

Sadie sat in the truck and grumbled in the August heat. She tapped her fingers in impatience on the steering wheel. Mentally she kicked herself for being such a marshmallow to let Gramps talk her into playing nursemaid to a stranger. Because she knew she'd be the one to help their guest, not her helpful grandfather. The meddler.

When the doors opened and presented the two conniving males, she took a deep breath before she got out of the truck. She needed to tuck her ire away. For now.

As she rounded the back of the truck, she glanced at Judson and felt guilty about her displeasure. He looked horrible. His features visible behind his bushy beard and long hair were paler than when he'd been inside. A fine sheen of sweat broke out upon his nose. Should he be dismissed from the hospital so soon?

She opened the back door before she turned to give him a helping hand from the wheelchair.

"I'll sit in the back, Sadie girl, if you'll help me up. Judson can ride shotgun."

She eyed her grandfather, her guard on alert. He was up to no good. She assisted him into the back seat. He settled himself and buckled his seat belt. She placed two fingers to her eyes and then pointed them back at him. She mouthed, "I'm watching you." He blinked at her and didn't utter a word.

She twisted to observe him. It appeared he hadn't moved a muscle. As she reached for the front passenger door, she noticed his clothing. She hadn't realized he still wore the tattered blue shirt. The garment had a tear on the right arm and was stained with blood.

He glanced down and grimaced. "I'm a sight."

She shrugged. "You'll get no arguments from me. But you can't go around town appearing like you've been beaten. Let me peek in the back to see if Gramps has a shirt you could borrow." She rummaged through the items on the floorboard. The only shirt available in the useless pile was pink. She smiled and held up her offering. "Sorry. I have this T-shirt, but I think it will fit, if you want to try."

He didn't reply but unbuttoned his shirt.

She swallowed. His movements were slow from the soreness of his limbs, but as she watched his actions they reminded her of a slow strip tease. Each button unveiled a chest pallid from lack of exposure to the sun, but she couldn't complain about the sculptured muscles he revealed. Had the afternoon sun and heat affected her? She wanted to fan herself. "Do you need help?" She tucked the pink top under her arm, reached out and assisted him with his shirt.

He sucked in a breath as her fingers grazed his chest. "I'm sorry. Did I hurt your shoulder?" He gave a negative shake of his head as she freed the last button. As he slid out of his stained garment a few older scars marring his well-muscled torso became exposed. Were those from prior gunshot wounds? Who was this man?

Not wasting any more time, she yanked the T-shirt over his head, covering up her unease, as well as the scars. "Are you okay? I'm sorry. I didn't mean to hurt you." She glanced up and her gaze met his intense one. His stare rivaled Clint Eastwood's squint. Had she ever seen eyes the color of his? "Do you need assistance into the truck?" He shook his head. "Okay, then. We need to go pick up your prescriptions before we can head home so both of you can rest."

She settled into the driver's seat and glanced at him. His face paled further, his complexion as white as a sheet. "Gramps, are you settled?"

She glanced into the review mirror and witnessed his nod. A few moments later, she parked in front of the pharmacy. He sat with a death grip upon the passenger seat, his knuckles white under the strain. "I shouldn't be long. You okay to stay in the truck?"

She flicked her wrist and consulted her watch. Ten minutes. She tapped her foot and wondered how much longer it would take to fill the prescriptions. She made a mental list of the chores to take care of when she got home. How was she going to take care of two invalids and handle her other responsibilities?

The ringtone from her cell phone interrupted her thoughts. She glanced at the display. Great. Just what she needed, a possible crisis at work. "Hello."

"Hi Sadie. It's Cliff."

"Hi. Is there a problem at the office?"

"First, how's your grandfather?"

"I've sprung him from the hospital and I'm in line to pick up some prescriptions. He has a sprained ankle, but no concussion."

"I'm glad it's not serious." He cleared his throat. "Can you come by the office on your way home? We've got a small glitch with the paperwork for the

Clark appointment."

She batted down a frustrated groan as she glanced at her watch again. "Glitch?"

"The file seems to have disappeared."

"Cliff, can you hold on a sec?" She paid for the medicine and thanked the clerk. She sighed and lifted the phone back to her ear. "I'll swing by."

"Thank you, Sadie. You're a life saver."

****

He pried his fingers loose from the leather cushion and worked them to get his circulation back into his hand. *What is this metal beast in which we've traveled?* He glanced out the window in wonder. She had lowered the glass by pressing a button before she continued inside the building in front of them. Hot air flowed around him as he stared at the different shapes, sizes, and colors of the same type of machines all about him.

Not one single thing appeared to be familiar. He stared in wonder at the buildings and the people.

He jumped as a hand grasped his shoulder. "Son, are you all right?"

His gaze swung to Walt's. "I must have died."

"I know everything seems strange."

His hand indicated his surroundings. "Everything I see…nothing is familiar." He ran a shaky hand through his hair. "Or as my life should be." He patted his shoulder. His gaze locked onto the older man's.

"We'll figure this out, son. Don't worry."

His throat burned as uncertainty raced in his mind. He couldn't seem to wrap his head around the situation in which he found himself. "What do you call this mode of conveyance we're riding in?"

"The vehicle is called a truck." He pointed out the

window. "The smaller vehicles are cars. It's our main mode of transportation."

"What makes them move?"

"They have motors and run on different types of fuel. I'm not much of a gear head, but I can try to explain and show you how they operate sometime."

He nodded but didn't understand the words. His world gone, in a blink of an eye. "Does no one ride horses anymore?"

He shook his head. "Not like they did in your time. These days it's a different type of horse power."

Chapter Seven

Sadie climbed into the truck and the conversation ceased abruptly as she clicked her seat belt. What had she interrupted? She glanced at the other occupants in the cab. "Judson, I got your medications. Cliff called while I waited on the pharmacy to fill your prescription. I need to go by the office. I don't think I'll be too long."

Gramps smiled. "Whatever you need to do, honey. We appreciate you taking care of us."

She sniffed the air. "I think I smell a rat." If she didn't know any better, her grandfather was sucking up. She squinted at him. Suspicion seeped into her mind before she started the vehicle.

"Did you say something, my dear?"

"Nothing." She focused on the traffic as the conversation ceased. An eerie silence filled the cab. She leaned over to turn on the radio to fill the quiet void. "Anyone have a request on what they would like to listen to?"

"You can pick the station. We'll listen to whatever, honey."

"Judson?" She hit the scan button and peeked in his direction. Sweat beaded his brow, even though the air conditioner blew upon his face. A frown creased his forehead. "Are you going to be sick?"

"No, ma'am."

She had to strain to hear his response. With a flick

35

of her wrist, she silenced the radio. Well, so much for avoiding the awkwardness.

A sigh of relief escaped her lips as she parked in front of Swanson's Law Office. "I'll leave the engine on so you'll have the air conditioner. I'm not sure how long this will take. Sit tight. I hope to be back in a jiffy."

The office bell rang above her head as she entered. The receptionist, Ann, glanced up from her computer and offered a smile.

"I'm sorry, Sadie. I didn't want to bug you, but the Clarks' appointment is this afternoon. I wasn't able to find their documents."

"It's fine, Ann."

"How's your grandpa?"

She chuckled. "Ornery as ever. I don't think the bonk on the head or the sprained ankle will keep him down for long."

She laughed. "I'm glad his injury wasn't serious."

She recalled the fright she'd experienced the day before and shuddered. "You and me both. I'll go fire up my computer and see if I can't find the Clarks' paperwork."

She tapped a finger on her desk as she waited for her PC to boot up. Her mind wandered to Judson. She'd wondered most of the morning what his story could be. Gramps didn't seem too concerned about the situation. Should she worry?

She dragged apprehension around of late like a ball and chain. A constant companion. Why couldn't she have good people skills like her grandfather? He could detect a rotten apple from a mile away. Unlike her. She closed her eyes as she reflected on his warning about

Troy. He'd cautioned her. But had she listened? He hadn't liked her boyfriend upon introduction. What a sorry state of affairs that ended up. She groaned. She shouldn't take all the blame for the ex's fiasco. Troy was the true villain in her sob story. Fickle son of a gun.

She shook her head. How could he have fooled her so easy? He'd been dating another woman in a nearby town while he wined and dined her. The dust had started to settle on their break up when the engagement announcement hit the local paper. Splattered in black and white for the world to see.

Idiot.

She stared at her computer a moment, not seeing the displayed words on the screen. She rolled her neck a few times before she clicked open a folder on her desktop. At least at work this wasn't her first rodeo. She'd learned to back up her documents in more than one place. Her boss, Cliff, had lost a whole day's work a couple of months ago. Thus, the precaution. She saved a copy of the documents into the client's folder and shut down her computer.

Minutes later she paused in her boss's doorway and smiled. He sat behind his desk with his reading glasses perched at an awkward angle on the tip of his nose. "Hi Cliff. The Clarks' information is back in their file."

Her boss took off his glasses and nodded. "Thank you, Sadie. I'm sorry you had to come by. How is Walt doing?"

She chuckled. "He's fine."

"That's good news."

She paused, she hated to inquire, but knew she had to. "I need to ask you for the rest of the week off. I'm sorry about this."

He stared at his calendar. "Are the documents for the Lewis appointment complete?"

"Yes, I finished them before I got the call from the hospital yesterday."

He formed his hands in a steeple. "I think we'll be fine. The schedule this week isn't hectic."

A sigh of relief escaped. "Thank you, Cliff. I appreciate the time off."

"I understand. You've got to take care of family."

Before she left she asked, "You will call me if you should need me, right?"

He grinned. "Doesn't today prove anything? We have you on speed dial. I hope Walt gets better soon."

"You know Gramps." She chuckled. "He springs back pretty quick from his escapades."

She bid Ann goodbye and made her way back out into the heat. Once settled in the truck, she spared a glance at her passengers before she put the truck in reverse. "Who's ready for a nap?"

"I don't know about Judson, but I could use one."

She plucked her T-shirt from her chest, allowing the air conditioner to flow under her hem. Oh, lots better. "I asked my boss for the rest of the week off so I can take care of you."

He stuttered and huffed from the back seat. "Now, honey, why did you go and do a fool thing like that? I have matters under control."

She tapped the wheel. "Well, let me see, Gramps. I left you alone for one afternoon." She held up a finger. "One. Have you forgotten about the emergency room and overnight stay at the hospital? Oh wait, that's where we just left. So, forgive me if I'm a little doubtful on your capabilities."

She glanced in the rearview mirror to see a shameful blush color her grandfather's cheeks. His lips were moving, but no sound emerged.

"Gramps, you know I hate when you grumble. Speak up. Did you have something to say?"

He cleared his throat. "I said I could handle the care of our guest."

She laughed at his foolishness. "Maybe he isn't the one I'm worried about." She stole a sly peek toward her front seat passenger. Did his lips quirk into a smile? She couldn't see past his facial hair, but she swore his eyes twinkled in amusement.

The cab fell silent once again as they traveled the last few miles to the house. As she made the turn into the drive she announced, "Home sweet home." Judson sat up straighter in his seat and studied his surroundings. She observed the barns, corrals, house, and imagined what he thought of their farm. She cringed at the obvious repairs sticking out like a sore thumb.

"Do you have horses?"

She smiled at his first show of enthusiasm since she first met him. "Yes. We have four at the moment."

"Maybe I can lend a hand with their care while Walt convalescences. I could work for my room and board."

She frowned. How long did he think he would stay? Didn't he have a home and obligations of his own? She shrugged off her musings. "I may take you up on the offer. But not today. You need to rest. Maybe tomorrow I can show you around."

She took Gramp's elbow to help him up the front steps. "Let's get you settled into your recliner. Then I will show Judson the guest room."

He removed her hand. "Quit fussing over me like an old wet hen. Go on. My recliner hasn't moved since I've been gone."

She mumbled under her breath, "Ornery cuss." She inquired of Judson, "Do you need to call anyone before you rest?"

"Call?"

"You know, use the phone." She chuckled. "Believe it or not we still have a land line in this day and age."

He stared at her a moment before he shook his head.

"Follow me, then. I'll bet you are ready for a nap."

He couldn't believe how drained the day's activities and confusion over his situation had worn him down. He followed her down a hall into a bedroom. He'd been amazed at his first glimpse of the Winters' farm. The house was built with different colored bricks, unlike the wooden home he'd grown up in. The barn and outbuildings were also impressive.

She opened a door and stepped inside. "I know it's not much, but you'll be comfortable."

He marveled at their home. Each room they passed through was furnished with items like he'd never seen. The bedroom he entered had soft blue painted walls. A big bed took up most of the floor. The room appeared inviting. Had he ever seen a room so grand? He sat down on the edge of the bed. The softness of the mattress amazed him. There couldn't be straw stuffed inside. He pondered a moment on what the bedding contained.

"I'm sorry it's a little stuffy in here. This room

isn't used much." She crossed to the window and pressed a button on a metal box protruding from the frame.

A cool breeze stirred the air. He stared, amazed at the machine.

"We have central heat and air, but the window unit helps when it gets so hot outside." She crossed back and stood in front of him. A soft smile settled on her lips. "I'm sorry this may sound bad, but you look like hell. I'll check your stitches and then I'll get out of your hair."

He eased the borrowed shirt over his head. As she leaned in, the same delicate fragrance he'd smelled earlier tickled his nose. He tried not to tense up as she examined his wound. Before when she'd helped with his shirt, her touch made his body tingle in a strange way. Once again at her feathered touch, a fluttering erupted in his belly. Had he ever been so aware of a woman? Did she also feel this attraction?

"I'll get a glass of water for you to take your medicine."

He eased down and rested his head upon the pillow. A tired sigh escaped. Total exhaustion dragged his eyelids down.

He blinked awake as a hand shook his arm.

"Judson? Lean up and swallow this then you can sleep."

He followed her instructions and struggled to keep his eyes open. "Ma'am?"

"Yes?"

He pointed at the pink shirt left on the table beside the bed. "I've been meaning to ask. What does Save the Ta Ta's mean?" A crimson hue crept up into her cheekbones. Had his question embarrassed her?

"Um." She fidgeted and wrung her hands. "You've never heard the expression before?"

He frowned. "No, ma'am. I can't say I have."

"My mother passed from breast cancer almost five years ago. Save the Ta Ta's is a slogan for breast cancer awareness."

He didn't grasp all she said, but one thing he did understand…she'd lost her mother. He lifted a hand and placed his over hers. "I'm sorry. I know what it's like to lose your loved ones."

She extracted her hand from his as she rose from the bed. "Gramps helped me through the hardest times. But I do still miss her."

"What about your father? Did he not help?"

She gave a cynical chuckle. "Oh, he helped when he left a long time ago. I don't even have a clue where he's wandered off to." She tilted her head and studied him a moment. "Do you need to take out your contacts before you take a nap?"

He rolled her question around in his mind. What were contacts?

She must have seen his confusion. "You don't wear glasses or corrective lenses?"

"No, ma'am."

A bemused expression crossed her features before she turned to leave. "I'll let you rest."

The strange words and images from the day fluttered in his mind as he closed his eyes. Would he still be here when he awoke?

Chapter Eight

Sadie paused before she exited the bedroom to glance back at the man lying in the bed, who seemed fast asleep. Was he as harmless as he appeared? She closed the door and squared her shoulders. Time to find out some answers to her questions. Gramps reclined in his favorite chair when she entered the living room. The television remote attached to his hand.

She waited for him to acknowledge her, but after a few moments she sank on the arm of the sofa and crossed her arms over her chest. "Are you ready to talk?"

"About what?"

She rose and paced a few feet. A glance over her shoulder proved he ignored her as he stared at the television. She pivoted and grabbed the remote from his hand.

"Hey."

She silenced the TV with a quick click. He didn't wear innocence well. She sighed and counted to ten in her mind. "I'm trying to understand something. What made you bring a stranger into our home? Do we know anything about him?" He met her glare head on and didn't utter a word. "Did you fail to notice they admitted him to the hospital with a gunshot wound, for cripes sake."

He brought his gnarled hand to his lips and shushed

43

her. "Shhh. Keep your voice down, he needs his rest."

Someone was off their meds…and it wasn't her. Words failed her for a moment. She sputtered before she squinted and drilled him with her best death glare. "That's it? You don't have anything else to say, but he needs his rest?"

"Now, Sadie girl. Don't go getting your dander up. I have my reasons why I dragged the poor boy home. You'll have to trust me on this one."

Boy. He was unbelievable. If the male in the other room were a mere boy, her body wouldn't be humming from the attraction she'd felt the minute she'd gotten close to check his stitches. Gramps wanted her to have faith in him. Yeah, well, she had a few issues in the trust department since the debacle with Troy. Maybe even before. She held the remote up in the air. "You're going to close your eyes and rest."

He grimaced. "But honey."

She wagged her finger in his direction, "Oh, don't honey me." She turned to leave. "I'll feed the horses and then I'll start our supper."

"Hey, you still have the remote."

She laughed as she stuffed the gadget in her back pocket. "No such luck. There isn't anything worse than a grumpy Gramps."

"Bossy woman," he muttered.

She turned and placed her hands upon her hips. "Did you have something to say?"

"Nope. Not a thing. Give the critters a scratch behind their ears for me."

The heat grabbed her as she stepped out onto the back porch. Fall couldn't come soon enough. She shook her head as she crossed the yard. Her annoyance with her grandfather diminished as she took a deep breath. She never stayed angry with him for long. But seriously…what had he been thinking? The crash to his head may have knocked a few reasonable marbles loose. She entered the barn and chuckled as the horses greeted her.

Thirty minutes later, she said goodbye to her four-legged friends and returned to the house. She checked on the patients. Both were sound asleep. She entered the kitchen to the sound of snores from the living room.

****

He awoke to the room drenched in semidarkness and a tantalizing smell filled the air. A quick glance about the room confirmed he still resided in the future. He sniffed in appreciation as his stomach growled. He rubbed a hand over his belly as he recalled he hadn't eaten much at the hospital. As he sat up, he wondered how long he'd slept.

He donned the borrowed pink shirt and followed the aroma to the kitchen, where she placed dishes on a table. "Are you sure, ma'am, I haven't died? Whatever you've cooked smells like heaven."

She gasped and swung around.

"Sorry, ma'am. I didn't mean to sneak up on you."

Her hand fluttered to her chest. "Goodness, you caught me by surprise. Supper is almost ready. Can you let Gramps know? He's through the doorway, asleep in his recliner."

"I can do that." He paused in the doorway. "I need to use the outhouse first. Can you point me in the right direction?"

A frown marred her forehead a moment before she answered. "The bathroom is across the hall from your

45

bedroom."

He stood inside the doorway and studied the modern privy. Everything indoors in one room, he liked the idea. The toilet he had experienced at the hospital. He liked the modern convenience. A tub took up a sizeable space and appeared to be permanent. The massive bath didn't seem to require to be hauled in and out.

In the other corner stood a glass enclosure. He tilted his head and studied it a moment before he tugged open the door and studied the knobs protruding from the wall. He stared in wonder as water jetted from the contraption overhead as he twisted one of the knobs.

After a few moments steam filled the room. He ran his fingers through the stream and drew back his hand. He stood amazed at the hot temperature. How did they boil the water and so fast?

He jolted from his reverie as a knock sounded on the door. "Judson? Are you okay?"

"I'll be out in two shakes of a lamb's tail." He switched the water off and took care of his business. He grasped the soap by the washbasin and brought the bar up for a quick whiff. A soft citrus fragrance tickled his nose. He smiled as he inhaled the pleasing smell. The scent was the same as Sadie's.

Walt stood outside the door as he opened it. A frown marred his brow. "You all right, son?"

He glanced about before he asked in a whisper, "What's the square glass contraption?"

The older man chuckled. "I thought you'd be impressed by the invention. A shower. After supper I will show you how to use it. Trust me, you'll love the experience."

He followed him back down the hallway. When they entered the kitchen, she turned and smiled.

"I wondered if I should send out a search party for you two. Go ahead and have a seat. I'm taking the lasagna from the oven."

He wasn't sure he'd ever eaten the dish before, but the aroma filling the air made his mouth water. "The food sure smells delicious, ma'am."

Walt piped in. "My granddaughter is a great cook."

She eyed him as suspicion crowded into her mind. Was he trying his hand at matchmaking? "You're a little biased because your cooking sucks."

"Indeed, it does." He patted his belly. "Didn't get my fashionably full figure from my meals."

She chuckled. "Well, before you dig in you need to say a blessing." She grasped her grandfather's hand and held out her other for Judson. He took it after a slight hesitation. His callused palm warmed her own. She concentrated on the words Gramps spoke, but she couldn't help comparing his hand to Troy's. Where her ex's were smooth, his were rough to the touch. To be honest, her last boyfriend oozed slick. In just about everything he did.

"Amen."

She picked up his plate and focused on the meal. "How much lasagna do you want? I warn you, you'd better get what you want now. Gramps doesn't leave much once he gets started."

Less than thirty minutes later she eyed the remnants of food in disbelief. A dish they usually had left over for days sat in the middle of the table demolished. Both men sat back in their chairs in contentment. "Glad to see your injuries haven't affected either of your appetites."

"Ma'am, that meal was the best I've enjoyed in my life."

She glanced at him and could feel a slow burn rise into her cheeks at the complete honesty reflected in his gaze.

Gramps shoved himself away from the table. "Judson, can I introduce you to the television in the living room?"

She rolled her eyes. "Oh yes, eat and run. The television is Gramps' favorite toy."

A puzzled expression flashed for a brief moment across his face. Before he could answer Walt rambled on. "Of course, I understand you're tired. I think the nurses poked and prodded you more than they did me last night." He shook his head and chuckled. "I'll go try to find some sleepwear for you and I'm sure you'd like to take a shower before you turn in for the evening."

He rose from his chair. She contained her annoyance. "I see how this works. Don't mind the mess. I'll tidy the kitchen."

Judson paused by the table as he rose. "I'd be happy to lend a hand, ma'am, on the cleanup."

Ah, at least one gentleman offered to help. She waved him away. "I've got this." She tilted her head and studied him a moment. "Would you like for me to wash your clothes? I'd be happy to. Just give your dirty laundry to Gramps and I'll throw them into the machine."

Chapter Nine

A twinge of guilt flickered through his conscience. He shouldn't have abandoned her to do the dishes alone. But he couldn't contain the excitement rushing through his system. He couldn't wait for the explanation of the glass square box in the washroom.

Walt stopped in the hall and opened a cabinet. "The clean towels and wash cloths are stored in here." He glanced back. "Would you like to trim your beard?"

He ran a hand over his face. When did he last shave? Or cared about his appearance? "I'm shaggier than a stray dog. Do you have a strap and straight razor?"

The older man chuckled. "The good ol' days of a fine shave. No, son. I have disposables. They are pretty simple to use. I'll go get you one."

Stepping into the bathroom, he studied his reflection in the giant mirror hanging above the washbasin. He didn't recognize the stranger who stared back. Earlier he hadn't taken the time to study his image.

His dark hair curled in utter chaos about his head. The beard and mustache weren't much better. Each sprang outward in wild disarray. The war resided in the forefront of his mind for so long, he hadn't cared about his appearance. Now he understood the mistrust he'd witnessed in her gaze and why she hid her fear of him.

49

Who could blame her? He frowned at his thoughts. Why should he care whether or not he scared her?

Walt stepped in behind him, his arms loaded down. "I have a toothbrush, toothpaste, scissors, razor, shaving cream, a pair of drawers and some sweats that will fit." He placed the items by the washbasin. "Ready for me to show you how to use the shower?"

His demonstration took a few minutes. He'd stood and watched, captivated by the other man's actions.

He stepped back. "I'll leave you alone to get cleaned up. The shampoo and soap are in the stall. Place your dirty clothes outside the door and I will take them to be washed."

After he deposited his clothes in the hallway, he fiddled with the knobs in the stall before stepping inside. A groan of appreciation eased from his lips as the water sluiced over his body. The combination of heat and coolness cascading over his body erased some of the tension. A constant companion he had since he awoke in the hospital.

He braced his hands on the smooth glass before leaning to rest his forehead against the flat surface. The agony of his unsuccessful mission weighed heavy on his mind and shoulders. The fact he had failed hadn't been far from his thoughts all day. The loss of lives and destruction occurring in Lawrence fell upon his shoulders.

What in the hell was he supposed to do now? He rolled his shoulders, shook off his glumness and retrieved the bar of soap. His thoughts focused on his other dilemma as he lathered his body. He didn't belong in this time. But did he belong anywhere?

As the temperature of the water grew tepid, he

shivered. How long had he been wool gathering? He shut the water off like he'd been shown. As he dried himself, he studied the stitches before he patted the area with the towel. Hadn't the doctor said to keep his wound dry? He couldn't recall the instructions. He hoped he hadn't caused any harm.

He flipped through the stack of clothes left for him but didn't see a pair of long johns. He lifted the items and decided the pair of drawers lacking legs were the under clothes. After he had donned the stretchy pants, he noticed there wasn't a shirt among the remaining items. He'd sleep better without one rubbing against his wound anyway. The fresh clothes felt wonderful. Better than his filthy uniform.

He stared into the mirror, his gaze unfocused. Where would he be if the Winters hadn't offered their hospitality? How could he pay them back for their generosity? He shook his head and brought his focus back to the task at hand. He picked up the shears, stared into the mirror a moment before he started to cut his beard.

****

Out of habit she checked Judson's pants pockets. In the left pocket, she found loose change. She glanced at the dates before she placed them on the dryer. A moment later she grabbed them off the slick surface. Did her eyes deceive her? Eighteen sixty-one. She shifted through the rest of the coins. Each had a date from the early Sixties. Why would he be carrying around antique coins? Wasn't that taking the reenactment life a little too far?

She set down the change and searched his right pocket. Something cool met her fingertips. She drew out an old beat up silver locket. She tossed the pants into the machine with an absentminded toss. A quick glance about proved the coast was clear. She opened the clasp. A black and white photo of a stunning woman was inside. Her eyes sparkled with life and happiness as she posed for the photo. Did he have a wife? He hadn't said anything about being married. But if the truth were told, he hadn't said much at all about himself.

"What ya got there, girl?"

She squealed and fumbled the locket a moment before the jewelry fell to the floor. It skittered across the linoleum a short distance before it stopped. Horror filled her. Had she broke the necklace?

Gramps laid the bloody shirt he'd retrieved from the truck near the laundry sink before he bent to pick up the locket.

She'd been caught red handed. Snooping.

He studied the photo. He ran a finger over the image before handing the piece of jewelry back. "A beautiful woman."

Where the metal had felt cool to her touch before, the piece now felt like fire. She snapped the locket shut. "Did he tell you he's married?"

He scratched his chin. "The matter hasn't arose."

She retrieved the money. "Why would he be carrying around antique coins?"

He whistled through his teeth as he shuffled through the loose change she'd placed in his palm. "I've only seen some of these in collector books."

"Exactly." She pointed to one a little different from the rest. "Check out this one. On the back it says one cent." She shook her head. "I don't understand. These must be worth a fortune. I don't understand why they'd be in his pocket like every day change?"

He ducked his head, not meeting her gaze. "I'm not sure, sweetie." He handed the coins back. "Can you put them in a safe place? I'm sure he would appreciate it if you did."

How could he be so nonchalant? Wasn't he even a bit intrigued by the coins?

"I'm bushed. I'm going to turn in for the night."

She studied his face and placed a hand on his arm. "Are you okay?"

He patted her hand. "Erase the frown. I'm fine."

She laid her head upon his shoulder. "I can't help but worry. You're all I got."

"I'm fine. My nap earlier didn't make up for the interruptions from the night before. Those nurses poked and prodded me all night long. Not my usual attention I get from females, if you know what I mean." He wiggled his eyebrows.

She groaned. "Gramps, you're incorrigible."

"You know you wouldn't have me any other way."

She chuckled. "You would be correct. Night."

"G'night."

He shuffled off mumbling about the awkwardness of the dang walking boot the doctor gave him for his foot. Where would she be if he weren't in her life?

Not dwelling on the morbid thought, she took care of the rest of the laundry. She retrieved the locket and glanced at the clock on the kitchen wall. She picked up Judson's pill bottle. Time for his next dose of antibiotic.

Halfway down the hallway she frowned when she realized he still occupied the bathroom. She inquired as she knocked on the door, "Judson? Is everything all right?"

Steam as thick as a fog edged its way out the door as it slid open.

"Oh." Heart pounding, she stepped back. He stood in the mist wearing a pair of her grandpa's sweats and nothing else. But that wasn't what had caused her heart to race. The scruffy wild facial hair had vanished. A few nicks graced his face. She marveled at what the removal of hair revealed. His features were striking. She held up the medicine bottle before she shook out a pill. "It's time for your next dose of medicine."

He didn't utter a word as he took the tablet from her.

She took a step backward. "Um, I can dress your wound once you've finished here."

"Sadie?"

She stopped in mid-retreat. "Yes?"

His gaze met hers before he pointed to his head. "Do you think you could cut my hair?" He shrugged. "You know. Give this mess on top of my head some order?"

She stared at the mass of thick curls and one errant lock brushing his forehead before she found her voice. "Sure. No problem. I haven't screwed up Gramps' hair. Yet." Her chuckle died in her throat at his serious expression. She placed a hand on his arm. "Hey, I'm only teasing."

A tentative smile twitched on his firm lips. "Thanks. I hadn't realized how out of hand my hair had gotten."

Awareness hummed in her veins at his stare. She yanked her hand back as if she'd been stung. "Come to the kitchen when you're ready."

She sank into a chair at the table. Where had her

mind been? Produce a half-naked man and her brain short-circuited. *You shouldn't be eyeing him like dessert.* But her mind screamed, *Bon Appetit. You don't know the first thing about him*, she admonished herself. *He could be worse scum than Troy.*

Moments later, he joined her in the kitchen. He still remained shirtless. Hadn't Gramps offered him one? She rose to retrieve the gauze and tape from the counter. "Are you ready? Let's dress your wound first." She indicated a chair. "Have a seat, and we'll have this done in a jiffy."

She leaned in to examine his injury. Fire radiated from her fingertips as she touched his bare skin. *Must concentrate*, she berated herself. *Damn hormones.* She cleared her now-parched throat. "As far as I can tell everything seems normal." His shoulder twitched as she applied the ointment and bandage. "I found your locket in your pocket before I put your pants in the wash." She pointed. "It's there on the table."

He picked up the locket. Silence hung on the air as he opened the piece of jewelry and ran a finger over the photo.

"The likeness is my mother."

Mother. His quiet words shimmied down her spine. Why did she feel a little elated he hadn't said wife? "She's beautiful."

He shut the locket with a forceful snap. "One of the many things this war took from me too soon."

She frowned. "Did she serve in the armed forces?"

His mesmerizing gaze met hers. Pain radiated from his gorgeous orbs. She still couldn't believe the color of his eyes. "I wasn't home when it happened." He swallowed. "If I hadn't been off on a scouting mission,

I could have saved her."

She waited, but when he didn't continue she inquired, "What happened?"

He struggled a moment before he answered. "She'd been out doing the wash. That's where our neighbor found her." His fingers caressed the necklace. "She'd been snake bit."

A shiver started at the top of her vertebra and shimmied all the way down her back. Snakes. She'd always had a fear, but never had known anyone who'd died from a bite. She placed a hand on his shoulder. "I'm sorry to hear about your mother. What was her name?" The heat of his skin had her drawing back.

"Elizabeth."

"A pretty name for a beautiful woman. What about your dad?"

A puzzled expression crossed his features. "What do you mean?"

Had his dad abandoned him like her father had deserted her? "Where's your dad?

He replaced the locket on the table. "He passed some time ago. I was young. My memories of him are few."

She bit her lip. She wasn't the only one who'd dealt with sadness in her lifetime. He'd told the officer he was twenty-nine. Not much older than her twenty-six years. "Do you have siblings?"

His lips quirked. "None I'm aware of."

A joke? He'd been so serious up to this point his humor surprised her. She chuckled and the sadness enveloping the room evaporated. She took a moment to study his long locks on top of his head. "I'm no professional hairdresser, but how do you want me to cut your hair?"

He waved a dismissive hand in the air. "Do whatever you think best for me to fit in."

She paused before picking up the comb and scissors. What an odd thing to say. What did he mean?

She retrieved a kitchen towel from a nearby drawer, draped it around his shoulders and caught a whiff of the soap he'd used in the shower. Funny, she'd never realized the scent of sandalwood and musk could be so enticing. Gramps sure didn't smell this appealing when he used the soap.

Her thoughts scattered the minute she touched his silky strands. Her hand shook. The act of cutting his hair shouldn't have felt so intimate. What wires in her brain had gotten crossed? She took a step back and regrouped. Just because she had a half-naked man at her fingertips didn't mean she needed to let her hormones take control. *Keep your mind on the task*, she admonished herself.

He sucked in a sharp breath as he became aware of her scent as she leaned near and ran her fingers through his hair. The sad thoughts dancing through his head in regard to his family vanished. A woman's caress. Soft. Gentle. He closed his eyes to savor the feeling. He hadn't enjoyed the touch of a beautiful woman in so long.

The moment she'd stepped close his brain turned to mush. The fragrance he'd come to recognize as hers tantalized his nose. The sound of the scissors snipping faded into the background as her fingers worked and threaded through his hair.

She shifted around to the front and nudged his knees apart. He swallowed hard as she slipped in between his legs to get closer to her task. He opened his eyes and his gaze settled on the soft curves of her breasts. The V of her shirt exposed her creamy flesh. Did she not realize how enticing a picture she presented? His nerves tingled as his body responded to her nearness. If indeed this travel in time were a dream, he didn't want to awake.

He shifted in his seat, uncomfortable with his body's reactions and his muddled feelings. His mind whirled grasping for conversation to take his mind off his thoughts. He jerked as she spoke. He cleared his throat. "I'm sorry. I didn't hear you."

She leaned down, met his gaze and smiled. "I'm almost finished. I noticed you were fidgety."

She wouldn't understand his restlessness. She'd slap him for sure at the direction his thoughts had taken.

Chapter Ten

About an hour later she crawled into bed, settled onto her side, and released a tired sigh. What a day.

The previous evening she'd tossed and turned with worry about Gramps and the stranger. The fact she had two invalids underfoot had worn her down. She hid a yawn. He hadn't talked much while she trimmed his hair. She'd felt most of the conversation fell upon her shoulders.

She reflected back to the photo in the locket. Elizabeth Stone's image revealed a beautiful woman. The picture puzzled her. She'd worn period clothes from a previous era. Had the photo been taken at one of those old-time places?

She twisted to her side and dozed as her thoughts eased off. Jerking awake, she leaned up on her elbow. She blinked a few times. What had awakened her? She listened for a moment. She shook her head and lowered her head back onto the pillow. She'd just settled when she heard another noise coming from somewhere in the house. She swung out of bed and approached her bedroom door with caution. She cocked her ear and listened before easing the door open. A slight creak emerged as she cracked it and peered down the hall. An agonized moan echoed in the silence. The noise had come from the guest bedroom. Was he in pain?

She paused in front of his door in indecision.

Should she interfere? Another groan came from the room. The sound made up her mind. She turned the knob and opened the door. Once inside she noticed the lamp by the bed put off a soft glow, casting an eerie shadow on the bed. He appeared asleep, but not in a peaceful slumber. He thrashed about as a nightmare consumed him. Suddenly he shouted, "No. Don't shoot. I've got to warn them.

He lashed about and another moan wrenched from his lips. She placed a hand on his shoulder and shook him in a gentle manner. "Judson."

"No." He shot up in bed and grabbed her hand.

She squeaked, surprised at his quick reflexes. "Judson. It's me, Sadie. You're safe. You were having a bad dream." He shook his head, released her hand and became aware of where he was.

He dragged a hand through his now short locks. "I'm sorry."

Distracted, she rubbed at her wrist and shrugged off his apology. "Are you okay?"

He shifted and brought the glass of water on the nightstand to his lips, drank his fill before he placed the cup back on the table. "I'm fine. I'm sorry I woke you."

Uncertainty nagged at her. Should she leave or ask about his nightmare? She sat on the edge of the bed. "It's okay. Do you want to talk about your dream?"

He covered his face with his hands and rubbed his eyes. "I found myself back on the trail. Staring down the barrel of Les's gun." He swallowed. "Just waiting for him or Earl to end my life."

She paused in offering a soothing hand upon his shoulder and frowned. His words bounced around in her brain. What? He knew who'd shot him. He'd lied.

To Gramps and herself. To the police. What other secrets did he keep? She rose and wrung her hands.

He didn't notice her distress as he continued to talk. His words didn't register as doubt ebbed into her mind. He couldn't be trusted after all. Had he brought danger to their farm? Were the men he described outside waiting for an opportune moment to take advantage of them? She almost stumbled as she backed away from the bed. "Well. You're safe now. You're not on the trail. Just a painful memory in the form of a nightmare. Try to get some rest."

He swung his legs out of bed and ran a shaking hand through his hair. The dream appeared so vivid and lifelike. He'd lived his failure all over again. He rested his elbows on his legs and stared at his trembling hands. He'd scared her half to death, if her hasty exit was any indication.

He sighed as he glanced at the closed bedroom door. All he'd done since he arrived was apologize. He needed to ask for forgiveness. Again.

Why was he here? Not at the Winters' home. But here, in the future? He'd been racking his brain most of the day after Walt had read to him the newspaper story about Lawrence. He still didn't have an explanation of what had happened to him.

He shook his head to clear the remnants of the dream. Could this just be an illusion? He lay back on the mattress and gazed at the night shadows dancing across the ceiling. He resembled those shadows, dark and hollow.

Chapter Eleven

The next morning, she sat at the kitchen table, a cup of tea cradled in one hand. The other held the business card Officer Williams had given them at the hospital.

Indecision tightened her gut. She didn't want to believe the worst of Judson, but she had to admit she didn't know him well. Did she call the officer and tell him her suspicions? The police should be aware of the situation. She shook her head. Why would he not tell the truth about such an important matter? Was he shot because of a drug deal gone wrong? Or worse? She couldn't imagine what he could be involved in or hiding.

She hadn't slept well as questions rattled around in her brain. Every time she'd closed her eyes, her mind would present another scenario. This is what Troy and his deception had done. She didn't trust anyone or anything. God, she hated this feeling.

"Good morning."

Startled out of her reverie, she watched Gramps make his way to the coffee pot. "Morning."

He poured a cup of coffee, smelled the aroma before he added a teaspoon of sugar. Once he finished stirring, his gaze met hers. Before he brought the mug to his lips, he frowned. "Are you not well?"

Great. Her appearance was awful if he noticed.

Clicking the corner of the card with her index finger she asked, "Did Judson talk to you about the shooting?"

He squinted at her. "Not exactly. Why?"

She shrugged and rose from the chair. "Something isn't right. He had a nightmare last night. Once he awoke he said he'd been staring down the barrel of Les's gun." She picked up her cell phone from the counter. "He knows who shot him. He told the officer he didn't."

"What are you doing?"

She sighed and entered her password to unlock her phone. "I think I need to talk to the police."

"No." He placed his cup on the counter, crossed the floor and grabbed the cell from her fingers.

"Gramps, we don't know what's going on." She lowered her voice. "For all we know he's some drug dealer and his deal went south."

He pocketed her phone in his shirt pocket. "That's not what happened."

Wait. Disbelief shimmied down her spine. He said he didn't know what had transpired, but his words hinted that he did. Could he be lying to her as well?

"Now before you go getting your panties in a wad, let me have my say."

She stared out the kitchen window. Her eyes misted. First her dad. Then Troy. Now her own grandfather. Couldn't she trust any man?

"I know you've been hurt by a lot of men in your life. Hell, I've even hurt you a time or two with my antics."

Wasn't that the truth. She wiped the stray tear from her cheek and faced him.

"I can't explain the circumstances right now. I'm

asking you to trust me." He ran a hand through his silver hair.

Why couldn't he give her an explanation? Her grandfather's instincts had never been faulty before. Should she let her fear or trust issues dictate the situation?

"Good morning."

Walt's gaze drilled into her own a moment before he greeted Judson. "Morning. Wow. Someone visited the barber after I retired to bed." He patted him on the back. "If I'm honest with you, it's quite an improvement. You're a nice-looking young man." He chuckled. "How'd you sleep?"

He glanced in her direction before he answered. "Not so well."

Hmmm…honesty. She hadn't expected the truth. "Would you like a cup of coffee?"

"Please."

"How do you drink your brew? Cream? Sugar?"

"No, black is fine. Thank you,"

She occupied herself by fixing a cup of coffee and struggled with her emotions. She drew in a deep breath and turned. "Judson, can I get you anything to eat? We have cereal for breakfast. I haven't had a chance to get to the store the last couple of days."

A confused expression crossed his features before he replied, "Just the coffee for now. Thanks."

"Are you sure? I think it's better to take your antibiotic on a full stomach." She opened a cabinet. "I could make you a PB & J sandwich. Unless you have a peanut allergy. Then I could scrounge something else up."

He exchanged a glance with her grandfather. When

Gramps gave a slight nod of his head, he replied, "The sandwich sounds great."

Huh? Gramps playing the role of puppet master? She just witnessed a new experience.

Twenty minutes later, he licked the tips of his fingers. The way he had consumed and enjoyed the PB & J, you would think he'd never had one before. "Would you like another?"

He shook his head. "No ma'am. But, I enjoyed the PJ & B."

She chuckled as she put away the peanut butter. "It's called a PB & J. I'm glad you enjoyed the sandwich. Are you ready for the tour and to meet the horses? I'll let you lend a hand, but only if you are up for the outing."

He leaned back in his chair. "I believe so, ma'am."

He made her feel older than her twenty-six years. "Sadie's fine. When you say ma'am I want to glance about for my mom."

"Sorry, ma'am. I mean Sadie. It's a habit."

She smiled at his hasty apology. "I'll go check on Gramps. I'm sure his butt is molded to his recliner and the remote planted in his hand, but I want to make sure he's settled before I take you out to meet the motley crew."

"Sadie."

She paused. "Yes."

His gaze met her own. "I'm sorry."

He exhibited remorse, but for what? Should she ask? "What are you sorry for?"

He drained his coffee and placed the empty cup in the sink. "For scaring you half to death last night."

She nodded and backed out of the room.

Chapter Twelve

Opening the barn door, gentle nickers greeted her and she smiled. "I believe the natives are restless. They expected their breakfast before now. Come on, I'll introduce you."

Stopping in front of the closest stall, she smiled at Judson. "This is Skittles." She cupped a hand to her mouth and whispered, "Don't tell the others, but she's my favorite."

His gaze took in the stall and then met hers. A frown marred his brow. "It's empty."

Had the knock on the head impaired his vision? He must be teasing. She chuckled. "No, it's not."

His gaze followed her pointing finger. "Holy Hell."

The curse made her and Skittles jump. He stumbled away from the stall. What little color he had obtained in the last twenty-four hours drained from his face.

"Judson?"

Gasping for air, he leaned on the barn wall for support. "What happened to the tiny filly?"

She frowned as she glanced from him to the horse. "I don't understand what you are asking."

He struggled with swallowing before he asked, "Where's the rest of her?"

"The rest of…?" A belly laugh grew and bubbled out from her lips. "Judson, haven't you ever seen a miniature horse before?"

He shook his head. "Are they all like this?"

She chuckled. "Like what?"

"Short. Squatty. Not all there?"

Was he serious? The laughter died an untimely death in her throat as she noticed his features. He had to be. No way could she misinterpret the panic mirrored in his eyes. Her precious babies were creeping him out.

She laid a calming hand on his arm. "Hey. It's okay." She guided him back to the stall and laid his hand on Skittles's head. "She loves to be scratched under her neck and behind her ear. Like any other horse you've met."

He stared at the miniature horse a moment before he leaned over to rub behind the small paint's ear. A true smile lit his face as Skittles closed her eyes, basking in the attention. A chuckle rumbled his chest. "Well, now. Aren't you a pretty little girl?"

Standing aside she pondered the alarm he'd displayed. No easy explanation could justify his reaction. In all appearances, he had never seen a miniature horse before. The prospect boggled her mind. Placing a hand on his arm, she led him to the next stall. "Here we have Twinkie. She's a tad chunky because she comes by her name naturally. She loves to eat Twinkies. I blamed Gramps for stealing my snacks, but we're onto her now. Guard your sweets, she takes no prisoners."

After the appropriate amount of scratching, they moved to the next pen. "This little guy Gramps named Backfire." She leaned over to whisper. "His name is appropriate because he's somewhat gassy and well, backfires…a lot."

A smile tugged at his lips, and he relaxed a little

more.

She led him to the next enclosure. "Last, but not least, we have Sinatra. Gramps named him after Ol' Blue Eyes himself. His favorite crooner." She smiled at the blue-eyed horse before turning her gaze to him. He wore a frown upon his brow. Why was he so serious?

He ran his fingers through Sinatra's mane. She could tell he loved horses by his gentle touch and handling of the animal. "You've truly never seen a miniature horse before?"

"No, ma'am. We had a pony when I was young, but he was a giant compared to these tiny guys."

She laid a tentative hand upon his arm. "Judson?"

He paused in petting the horse and met her gaze. "Yes."

She took a moment to gather her thoughts. Where did she even begin? She wanted answers. Questioning Gramps had led her to a dead end. Dare she try her luck with him? "What's going on?"

The frown marring his brow deepened. "Ma'am?"

She took a step back, crossed her arms and met his gaze. "I want you to spill."

He shook his head. Confusion appeared on his features. "Spill?"

She struggled to control a groan of frustration. Were all men obtuse? Or just the ones who resided in her home? "Yes. I want to know what the hell is going on. Now."

His gaze swung away as he shifted in an uncomfortable fashion from one booted foot to the other, before he turned and sat on a nearby hay bale.

"You won't hyperventilate, will you?" She sat by him and waited.

He shook his head. "I can't."

"You can't what? Hyperventilate?"

He jumped to his feet and ran a hand through his hair. He spread his hands wide. "Explain. Anything. Not a damn thing."

Obstinate men. She shook her head in disappointment as she picked up a nearby feed bucket. "I'll take care of the animals. Go on back to the house. I can show you the ropes some other time."

****

She told herself she wasn't hiding out. Retail therapy always worked in the past. But not today. Her brain wasn't focused on shopping. For herself anyway. At the moment, her treatment had gone off and left.

She'd left Gramps and Judson back at the house in hopes of them taking a nap. She shuddered at the thought of what they may be doing. Gramps's antics challenged her on a daily basis. But she was used to his adventures. The unknown of what trouble followed Judson brought on a new level of anxiety. What problems would he bring to their farm?

She stood in front of a store window, her mind whirling. The morning events in the barn replayed like a movie in her head. Judson had taken a ride on an emotional rollercoaster. Panic. Shock. Exasperation. Frustration. She'd witnessed every aspect of his distress in such a short span. What was he hiding? She wasn't the only one suffering from trust issues. He had them in spades.

She shook her head and stared at the shirt catching her attention. The polo the mannequin sported was an aquamarine. The exact hue of his eyes. Judson. Why couldn't she keep her thoughts away from him?

She tilted her head and took a bite of the chocolate chip cookie she'd purchased. Nodding, she decided why not. He couldn't wear his reenactment wear every day until he goes home. Now could he?

Upon entering the store, she made her way to a stack of shirts. She flicked through them and bit her lower lip. What size did she need to buy? She held up each and studied them. Soon her hands were laden with several vibrant colored shirts.

"Miss, do you need a basket?"

She turned and smiled at the clerk. "I wandered in for one item. But as you can see, I've deviated from the plan. I guess a basket may be a good idea."

"Let me know if I can help you in any way."

She contemplated the store. "Men's jeans?"

The clerk smiled. "Follow me. They are over here against the wall."

Soon her basket held the shirts, a couple of pairs of jeans, socks, and a bag of boxer briefs. She shook her head bemused. Why spend her hard-earned money on a man who could be a criminal of some kind? She rejected the thought as soon as it entered her mind. He may not be telling the truth, but she believed he wasn't involved in any criminal activity. She sent a quick silent prayer she wasn't wrong.

"Hi, Sadie. I thought it was you."

The deep voice from behind made her cringe and roll her eyes skyward. She hadn't expected to hear her rat-fink ex's voice. Not shopping anyway. Why now? The day kept getting better and better. She forced a smile to her lips and swiveled to face Troy. A second or two passed before she realized he wasn't alone. This must be the famous fiancée. She paused struggling to remember her name.

"Sadie, this is Tracy."

Ding, ding. Now she remembered. "Hi, Tracy."

An awkward silence ensued as his gaze roamed over her and the items in the basket. His smile disappeared as he frowned and glanced at his watch. "Is today a holiday?"

Maybe she'd lost her mind. His question stumped her. "A holiday? No, why?"

He splayed his hands to encompass the store. "Shouldn't you be at work?"

The censure in his voice grated down her spine. "Well, not that it's any of your business, but Gramps had an accident this week and I'm off work for a few days."

"Is he all right?"

She turned toward the other woman. She'd been quiet up to this point. "Thank you, Tracy, for asking. He has a sprained ankle and will be back to his spry self in a matter of days."

His brow lifted as he examined the items in her basket once again. "Then you're out shopping for Walt? I wouldn't have pictured him as the silky boxer brief type."

Her chin inched up and the imp in her replied, "You'd be correct. They aren't for him." She smiled inwardly; let him chew on that bit of information. "If you will excuse me, I need to get home." A hand on her arm stalled her.

"You're looking good, Sadie."

She would have felt pleasure at his compliment not so long ago. Now, his praise left her chilled. "Thank you." She couldn't reciprocate. He didn't deserve her flattery.

"I'm glad I got to see you."

She nodded but refrained from commenting. What did he expect? A warm hug and let's do dinner some time? Just the three of us.

As Sadie stood in line, her neck hairs stood at attention. Either Troy or Tracy's gaze drilled holes in her. It took control not to turn around to find out. She'd bet the culprit was his fiancée. She didn't know what Tracy had to be envious about. She was the one sporting the diamond engagement ring.

Chapter Thirteen

"Dag gum it. I hate this new technology mumbo jumbo."

Judson watched as Walt fiddled with the box he called a laptop. They sat at the kitchen table hoping to get some answers before she was back from town.

"I don't know how she can work on one of these contraptions every day. These computers are frustrating as hell."

He smiled as another curse word escaped his mouth. He'd lost count of how many colorful words escaped from his mouth over the course of the afternoon.

"Got it. Finally."

He leaned over the other man's shoulder to study the colors and words. "What is goo…goog?"

"Google. It's a search engine, or so Sadie told me. You put in the information, and it helps find what you're hunting for. Let's search the Eleventh Kansas Cavalry first."

As the afternoon progressed, his head pounded with a furious headache. "Enough." He stood and strode to the kitchen window. He rubbed the back of his neck in frustration. Everything they searched only provided more questions without answers. Some of the images they'd encountered were familiar, but they had yet to find why or how he had travelled from the year eighteen sixty three. His total existence was in limbo.

"Son?" He placed a hand on his shoulder.

He bowed his head and moaned. "What the hell happened to me?"

"I've never thought of time travel before. The possibility boggles my mind." He scratched his chin. "The reality of your situation puts the science fiction books I've read to shame."

His gaze met the older man's. "I'm surprised you believe the words I've been spouting."

"I'm a good judge of character, son. I can tell a good apple from the bad, and I can't say why, but what you've said rings true."

He ran a hand through his hair, tousling his already disheveled locks. "Sadie asked me this morning in the barn to explain my situation. I froze. What can I tell her that doesn't make her distrust me more than she already does? Hell, I don't believe what happened."

He patted him on the back. "She comes by her trust issues honestly."

"I figured as much when she told me she didn't know the location of her own father."

Surprise flittered across his face. "She told you about her dad?"

He shrugged his shoulders. "Not in depth. She mentioned him briefly when she told me about her mom."

His lips curved into a sad smile. "My daughter, Jillian. She was such a live wire. I had a hard time watching her fight her battle with breast cancer." He turned away and cleared his throat. "I still miss her cheery laugh."

"I'm sorry for your loss." He watched Walt close

the machine they'd used to find information. "What happened to your wife? If you don't mind me asking."

A sad smile crossed his face. "My sweet Grace. She had a bum ticker." His gaze met his. "Her heart gave out on her."

"It's you and Sadie then?"

The sadness disappeared as he chuckled. "The two musketeers. Sadie and I are good for each other, don't let her convince you otherwise."

"I can see that, sir."

The older man placed a hand on his shoulder. "Judson?"

"Yes, sir?"

"Could it be you were meant to be here? In this time? Place?"

He stared into the other man's intent gaze. "What are you saying?"

"The reason we didn't seem to find any answers for your existence in eighteen sixty-three is because you belong here."

He stared out the window. She had let the little horses out into the corral before she'd left to go into town. They ran and frolicked in the afternoon sun. Was what he said possible? He'd gotten a second chance at life? Away from all the pain and suffering of the war?

What was back there for him anyway? His parents were both dead and he didn't have any other family or a woman sharing his life.

"Give the idea some thought. I'll help you any way I can."

"Thanks, Walt."

****

With the air conditioner and radio turned up, she

sang along to a Blake Shelton tune. She tapped her fingers on the steering wheel, and her thoughts wondered back to the store. Why had Troy even approached her? Didn't he realize the hurt he caused by his two-timing?

She nibbled on her lower lip. The heartache and embarrassment hadn't seemed so acute today when she faced him. Maybe, just maybe, her heart was on the mend.

She smiled as she recalled his face when she told him the boxers weren't for Gramps. Priceless. Score one for her team.

Twenty minutes later, hands laden with sacks of groceries, she entered the house. "Gramps?"

"I'm in my recliner watching TV, honey."

She placed the bags on the counter. "Can you come and put away the groceries? I've got to get a few more bags."

Seconds later, he shuffled into the kitchen. "Did you buy enough to feed an army?"

"Almost. Between you and Judson, I feel like I'm feeding a whole platoon." She glanced behind him. "Where is our guest?"

He shrugged his shoulders. "I fell asleep in my recliner. My guess is he's resting as well."

She nodded as she finished emptying a sack. "Can you put the food away?" The screen door banged as she exited to the porch.

Shading her eyes, she glanced at the corral. She smiled at the serene scene. She'd found him. Backfire, Sinatra, Twinkie, and Skittles were all lying down in a semi-circle and his head rested against Sinatra's belly. Was he asleep?

She crossed the yard and propped her chin on her arms as she leaned against the corral's top rail. Indeed, he was napping. A grin tipped her lips as a gentle snore escaped from his lips. Her babies rested in contentment around the man as he slept.

She hated to disturb his slumber, but if she left him to bake in the sun, he'd be miserable. He had a gunshot wound. Sunburn on top of his injury asked for trouble. Skittles spotted her and nickered. The mini met her at the gate. "Hi, baby." She ran a hand over her back. "How pretty you look. Someone groomed you, huh?"

He hadn't moved an inch. She studied him. The lines of tension had eased in his slumber. The wild hair, mustache, and beard he had sported had disguised a rugged, nice-looking man. Her gaze was drawn to his lips. Would they be as firm as they looked?

She admonished herself. *Stop it. You don't need a man in your life's equation.* Kneeling down, she nudged his shoulder with her hand. "Judson."

A frown marred his brow before his eyes popped open and stared at her unfocused. "What?" He sat up and shook his head.

"I didn't want to disturb your nap, but you'll get sunburnt, if you haven't already."

He ran a hand down his face. "Guess I dozed off."

She smiled at his timid admission. "If the snore I heard was any indication…you'd be correct."

A chuckle rumbled in his chest as he cast a boyish glance in her direction. "Sorry."

"You don't need to apologize. You've had a rough few days."

He nodded his head in agreement. "You've no idea."

She had to lean in to hear his murmured words. "You know, I'm surprised Sinatra let you lie on him. He's been a little stubborn in his training."

He frowned. "Training?"

She waved a hand in the direction of the horses. "I've taken each through a course to get them ready to be a therapy horse. Sinatra is my latest acquisition. He's been a little difficult."

He ran a hand over his back. "I think we are kindred spirits. We understand each other."

A calm radiated from him he hadn't displayed before she'd left for town. What had changed? She studied his bent head. "Hey, I appreciate your help combing these guys. I'm afraid I've neglected them over the last few days. I feel like I've run in circles since Gramps's accident and his time in the hospital."

His gaze met hers. "I'm sorry. I've added to your daily chores."

His eyes were gorgeous. She stared a moment before shaking her head to focus back on the discussion. "Hey, I didn't mean to suggest you're a burden. You're welcome to stay here as long as you need."

A sigh escaped his lips, and his shoulders sagged in relief. She wanted to ask questions but knew she'd met a brick wall the last time she'd tried. She rose and stuck her hand out to help him up. "Come on. Want to see what I bought in town?"

He accepted her assistance and rose to his feet.

She backed up a step once she realized how close he stood. Heat from the sun and his body radiated toward her.

"I repaired the loose boards in the barn and some

out here on the corral. I'll finish mending the rest of your repairs when the temperature is cooler outside."

She turned toward the gate. "I appreciate your help. Those tasks were on Gramps's honey-do list. He hadn't gotten to them." She chuckled. "He will be glad you took care of them."

His answering smile caused her to pause. *Do not focus on how his smile released a dozen butterflies in her stomach.* She shook her head in an attempt to erase her errant thoughts. This was Troy's fault. He'd rattled her. She couldn't let herself act on an attraction she started having for a man she didn't know.

She could feel his gaze on her as she crossed the yard. She glanced over her shoulder and caught his gaze checking out her backside. Warmth spread down her spine. Did he fight the same attraction that plagued her?

She dragged a few sacks from the truck. Surprise filled her as her load was taken from her hands. "You don't have to help carry in the groceries. I don't want you to hurt your shoulder."

He examined the items in his hands. "I've carried heavier. Besides, it's the least I can do, ma'am. You've put a roof over my head and fed me. And don't worry about my injury. I'm healing fine."

"Well, okay. If you're sure. I don't want you to overdo things."

Upon entering the kitchen, she noticed her laptop on the table. Hadn't she used her computer last in the living room? Had Gramps used the machine again? Or Judson? Should she ask what they'd been up to while she was away? She glanced at both men as they unpacked the groceries. Would she get a straight answer if she did? "I'm glad both of you were able to

N. Jade Gray

get some rest while I was out." A guilty expression passed between the two men. What did the silent message mean?

Walt scrubbed a hand under his chin. "A bit."

Another fleeting glimpse passed between the two men. Yep, the exchange said it all. They'd been up to no good. "Judson, I bought a few items for you to wear while I was in town. I know I may have gone overboard, but you can return what doesn't fit."

At his silence, she turned. His cheeks were flushed, and his gaze didn't meet her own. "Are you feeling all right? You didn't overdo after all, did you?"

He shook his head as if coming from a trance and produced a tentative smile. "I don't believe so."

She placed the bags of clothes in front of him before retrieving a pitcher of lemonade from the refrigerator.

"What's this?"

She placed a glass in front of him as she took a chair adjacent him. "Well, since retail therapy wasn't working for me, I decided to get you a few things."

A strange expression crossed his face before he cleared his throat. "Sadie." He thrust the bag away. "I can't accept this."

Hurt tingled up her spine. "Why not?"

His gaze caught hers. "I don't have any money to pay you back."

She'd wounded his pride. She hadn't meant to. "We won't worry about you paying me back at the moment. We will call my purchases an exchange for the things you fixed on the barn and corral this afternoon."

Gramps raised a celebrative hand into the air. "Whoop. I say any chores I can get out of, power to you."

She and Judson laughed in unison, easing the tension in the air.

She scooted the sack back in front of him and patted his hand. "Thank you in advance for the help with the repairs to the corral and barn."

He stared into her eyes a moment before he gave her a brief nod. He drew his hand from under hers and reached into the bag. Dragging each item out, he inspected each.

Walt leaned over the pile on the table and whistled through his teeth. "How come you've never bought me drawers like those?"

A wave of heat reached her cheeks. "Hush." She rose and crossed to the refrigerator to refill her glass of lemonade. Why hadn't she purchased regular boxers? The imp present when Troy confronted her felt foolish now.

She saw her grandfather pile the items into his hands. "Well, go ahead, son. Go try on your new duds."

She sipped her drink and almost choked when Gramps broke the silence after he retreated from the room.

"I wish I had some silky underwear."

She closed her eyes and counted to three. Sometimes dealing with her grandfather was like taking care of a toddler. "I'm sorry, I didn't realize you would like to give them a try."

"Well, now you do."

She shook her head. "Noted. I'll be sure to put them on your Christmas list." She couldn't believe this conversation.

Moments later, he returned in the polo matching

his eyes and the Levi's she'd bought.

He wiped his hands down his thighs. "Are these denims supposed to be this tight?"

Oh, yeah buddy, her mind screamed. She'd found him attractive after his hair cut and his facial hair had disappeared. But the clothes. Wow. The shirt and jeans she'd chosen showed off his physique he'd hidden inside those baggy clothes he'd worn. She shook her head to dislodge her errant thoughts. A moment later, she realized he stared at her as he waited for an answer. "We can return them and get a different size if you'd like."

Gramps crossed the floor, and clasped his shoulder. "Son, I hate to break the news to you, but a lot of young men wish they could wear denims like you do." He winked. "Me included. I'd love to drive the ladies wild, but I have such a bony butt."

"Gramps."

He held up his hands in the air. "I give. I'm going to relax in my recliner. Care to join me, Judson?"

"No, thank you, sir. I think I will finish the nap I started outside."

As they left the kitchen, she shook her head and smiled. Her grandfather was one in a million.

She stowed the last of the food away and slipped her computer under her arm. In her bedroom, she sat cross-legged on her bed and opened her laptop. Gramps. He was the culprit. She could tell by the sticky spots on some of the keys. He snacked while he worked his magic.

He didn't understand technology. He would be irritated to know she kept an eye on the items he searched. She tried her best to head off a disaster he may cause before it happened. Lord help her if he ever figured out how to clear his browser history.

She clicked on the down arrow and frowned at the items searched. The Eleventh Kansas Cavalry/Infantry. The burning of Lawrence. Quantrill Raiders. Time travel. The final search was for an obituary for Judson Levi Stone.

She glanced up from the screen and gazed across the room. A wave of confusion rushed through her brain. What did the searches mean? The anniversary of the raid on Lawrence would occur in a few days. But the other subjects didn't make sense. Why would they hunt for an obituary for Judson? He was right here in their guest bedroom. And, boy, if he was dead, she was a super model.

What crazy idea had he talked her grandfather into believing? She shook her head. Time travel? Really? How on earth did the subject figure into this? She glanced at the clock on the wall. The library would be closed soon, so she couldn't do further research today. Tomorrow she would investigate further. Now was the time for her to be proactive to find answers.

Both men were quiet at dinner. She attempted conversation, but extracting teeth would have been easier. The only good thing about the evening was the gloom from the afternoon hadn't affected anyone's appetite.

Placing the last dish into the dishwasher, she noticed the other occupants in the room hadn't moved a muscle. "Let's adjourn this spirited party to the other room. Anyone up for a game?"

Gramps nodded. "Some light entertainment may be what the doctor ordered. If we don't play a game, maybe we could watch a movie. As long as you don't pick a chick flick."

"Spoil sport." Entering the living room, she crossed over to stop in front of a shelf laden with DVDs.

She'd trailed her fingers over a few titles.

"How about the comedy about the crazy doctor who traveled to the old west?"

She glanced back at her grandfather.

"You know, the one that had a fancy car."

She frowned. Did he mean the time travel movie with Michael J. Fox? He was like a dog chewing on a bone. She flipped her hand toward the movies. "I'm sure Judson has seen the movie a million times. Don't you want to see what else we have?"

He crossed his arms. "Well, I haven't seen it in awhile."

Act like a two-year-old much? She tried not to roll her eyes as her gaze met Judson's. "Is that one okay?"

He stared at her for a couple of seconds without a blink before he nodded. "Yes, ma'am. It's fine."

They were two peas in a pod. She turned and placed the DVD in the player. "Okay, remote master, play whenever you're ready. I'll go pop some popcorn. I will be back in a jiffy."

Judson stared in wonder at the picture appearing on the black box in front of him.

Walt leaned forward in his recliner, glanced over his shoulder, and whispered, "This invention is called a television. It's a form of entertainment. I spend too much time watching the tube."

He leaned forward on the couch. "How do they get those people into the black box?"

He chuckled. "This is another area I can't expound

upon. Like the computer, I can't explain the technology mumbo jumbo."

He was captivated. Amazed and entranced, he didn't hear her join him on the couch. Soon he understood why he'd picked the story. The older man had travelled through time. But according to Walt, the tale was to entertain. Things like what he was facing didn't happen in real life. Did they?

The story ended with the Doc staying in the period in which he'd found himself. Another reason he chose to watch this story, to make a point? He asked him a question, but the old man was fast asleep, leaning at an awkward angle to one side in his chair.

A quick glance in her direction proved she was fast asleep as well. One hand was tucked under her head as she leaned against the arm of the couch. Her dark eyelashes rested against her cheeks. An angel at rest.

"No need to wake her. Can you carry her to bed?"

He startled at the other man's quiet words.

Walt hoisted himself from his chair and leaned over to silence the black box. "I'll get the lights."

He stood, bent over, and lifted her into his arms. She sighed and nestled her head against his shoulder. Her breath caressed his skin. He cradled her closer. A light fragrance from her hair tantalized his nose. He dragged in a deep breath and shook his head. His fascination for the petite woman in his arms was growing. He couldn't afford to become attached. Not as his mission and future hung in the balance.

Walt opened her bedroom door and flipped on the overhead lantern. "Good night, son. Sleep well."

"Night." He took her into her room. It was larger than the one she'd given him. Feminine touches were displayed throughout the area. He crossed over to her bed and gently laid her down. A sigh escaped her mouth, and he smiled. His smile slipped as he studied her lips. An overpowering urge to lean down and bestow a kiss shook him. He admonished himself and backed away. A kiss would only complicate his situation further. He doused the lights with a quick flick of his hand and retreated from her room.

Chapter Fourteen

She stirred as a bird chirped outside her window. Someone was a happy camper this morning. She glanced at her bedside clock. Not quite seven. She frowned as she stretched. When had she crawled into bed? The last thing she remembered was observing Judson as he watched the movie. His fascination was of a young child seeing cartoons for the first time.

A glance at her sleep attire proved she still wore the clothes from the previous day. She must have fallen asleep on the couch. Someone had put her to bed last night. Gramps hadn't been able to lift her since her teenage years. That left one other person. Judson.

She placed her hands behind her head and stared at the ceiling. A couple of nights ago he'd arrived at the emergency room disheveled and dressed in a Union uniform from the Civil War era. At the time, she'd put the outfit down to a practice for a reenactment for the anniversary of Quantrill's Raid. Could the clothes mean something different?

The coins she'd found in his pants' pocket and his mother's locket served to be another mystery. For some reason, Gramps was fine with the secrecy surrounding their guest. Did he believe he'd travelled through time?

The idea seemed a little farfetched. Even for her adventurous grandfather. But then she had to consider his strange reactions to her miniature horses and his other responses to a lot of their modern conveniences.

Maybe her goal for the day should be research of her own. She still had a few days off from work. Her top priority was to find answers.

Thirty minutes later she was in the kitchen fixing French toast when the home phone rang. "Hello."

"Ms. Winters?"

"Yes?"

"Good morning, Officer Brody Williams here."

An unwelcomed chill made its way down her spine. "Good morning, officer. What can I do for you?"

"I want to stop by this morning to visit with Mr. Stone."

Was this the call she'd dreaded? "Do you have a lead in his shooting?"

"Our office has received some new information and I need to talk to him about the events of the other night."

She bit her lip. Now was the time to tell him her fears, to voice the doubts and concerns she juggled in her head. After what she'd found on her laptop, she held her tongue. "Well, we were getting ready to sit down to breakfast."

"That's fine. I won't be able to get to your place until around nine."

She glanced at the time on the microwave. "I'll let Judson know. Bye."

She fiddled with the cordless phone a moment before she headed down the hall to knock on his door. After a few moments without an answer, she knocked again. She turned the knob and called out, "Judson."

The bed was neatly made and the room empty. She turned and noticed the same could be said about the bathroom across the hall. Where was he? She retraced her steps back to the kitchen. Movement caught in her peripheral vision had her stepping toward the window. He crossed the yard strolling toward the barn. His steps seemed a little livelier this morning. Maybe the funk he'd suffered from earlier deserted him.

She turned, switched off the burner on the stove and removed the pan from the heat. The screen door slammed behind her as she made her way across the yard. Humidity already hung heavy in the air. The day would be another scorcher.

A male voice spoke in soft tones within the confines of the barn walls as she entered. Should she let him know of her presence? She peeked around the corner to witness him sitting on a hay bale with a knife in his hand whittling on a piece of wood. Skittles stared with an extreme interest nearby.

"Has anyone ever told you what a great listener you are?"

She smiled at the one-sided conversation.

His gaze roamed over the horse. "Aren't you the darndest thang?" He paused on his project to glide his hand down one of the mini's legs. "God does have a sense of humor, doesn't He? How else can He explain you?" He shook his head. "You're smaller than our pony I had growing up. He was always in Ma's garden. She used to fuss every time she'd catch him munching on her veggies." He chuckled at the memory.

Guilt crept up her spine on her blatant eavesdropping. She cleared her throat to announce her presence. "Judson?"

He turned at the sound of his name and smiled. "Good mornin'."

She froze. The smile he'd bestowed upon her reached his eyes. Little flutters erupted in her stomach. *Now, cut it out. She admonished herself.* Now was not the time to go gaga over a handsome man.

With a shake of her head, she cleared her thoughts. "Officer Williams phoned. He will be by at nine to talk to you."

The happiness drained from his features. He glanced away, but not before she witnessed the worried frown upon his brow. "I lent a helping hand. I'm almost finished giving the horses their breakfast."

She glanced at the piece of wood resting by his thigh. "Do you like to carve?"

He picked up his project and ran a hand over where he'd already shaped. "I enjoy the finished piece. What the wood becomes."

She leaned in to observe his actions. "Do you know what it will be?"

He pointed to his head. "In my mind, the end likeness will be of this little filly."

Skittles sensed they talked about her and let loose a big whinney.

She laughed at the horse and ruffled a hand through her mane. "I can't wait to see how your whittling turns out. Breakfast is almost ready. Do you need a hand here?"

"No. I've got it. I'll be along in a minute."

He stood and watched her exit from the barn before he led the mini back into her stall. His stomach erupted into a thousand butterflies as dread filled his thoughts. What did the officer want? Would he take him away from the Winters' home and arrest him?

He took his time, paused at each stall, and

scratched the horses behind their ears.

Since he'd gotten over the shock of how small they were, they were adorable. Each had a character and personality of their own. He missed his horse and riding him, but he could see the charm of these little fellows as well.

He'd awoken before dawn renewed. Like he had a new lease on life. Walt's words played in his mind and he'd been ready to embrace what the future held. Then she had said the officer wanted to speak to him and his whole peace of mind crumbled.

His feet felt like weights as he entered the house. He washed his hands in the kitchen sink, then settled in a chair at the table next to Walt.

"Why so glum?"

He glanced at him. "The officer from the hospital is coming by the house to talk to me."

"Oh." The older man patted his hand. "I'm sure there's no reason for concern."

He nodded, but his anxiety didn't dissipate. He enjoyed the meal she prepared, but his nerves were on edge. When the knock he'd been expecting sounded at the door an hour later, he tensed.

She left the room to answer the door.

He rubbed his sweaty palms down his pants leg. He rose as the officer approached.

"Good morning, Mr. Stone."

"Mornin."

She hovered nearby. "Officer Williams, can I get you a cup of coffee?"

"That sounds great, Ms. Winters, but I won't have time to enjoy it." He turned to him. "I wanted to come by and let you know we're closing your case. Once Mr.

Winters called yesterday and told me the circumstances, we understood your hesitancy to talk."

He frowned, puzzled at the officer's words. He didn't understand the position he found himself, how did Walt explain the situation?

"Mr. Winters described the accident and how you didn't want to get the responsible party into trouble." The officer gestured with his hand. "The organization responsible for the reenactment should know about the incident and their liability in keeping the reenactors safe. Live ammo is not allowed. Once he told me the organizer's name, I gave them a call and we talked through the ramifications of the incident. The guilty party will be reprimanded and not allowed to participate in another reenactment until he's educated on gun safety."

Walt stepped forward and put a hand on his shoulder. "Judson didn't want to name names and get anyone in trouble, but I'm glad we can put this behind us."

The officer nodded and placed his hat back upon his head. "Mr. Winters, I appreciate your assistance. I will finish the paperwork and close your file." He turned and at the door bid them all a good day.

He stared at the back of the retreating man. What had happened? Had Walt lied to the law? He stared into the other man's intent gaze. "What did you do?"

He shrugged his shoulders. "What needed to be done."

"But…"

"Son, this wouldn't have gone away without an explanation. I gave them a reason that makes sense. Take advantage of this, and live your new life."

She sagged against the kitchen counter as Gramps ambled from the room. Judson's eyes appeared misty as he excused himself and strolled outside.

Shock settled down her spine. What had her grandfather done?

She followed him into the living room and watched him settle into his recliner. A surge of anger overtook her at his blasé attitude. "What the hell have you done?"

His gaze flashed fire. "Don't you yell at me, young lady."

She ran a hand through her hair. "Gramps. Did you or did you not commit an illegal act?" She paced between the couch and his chair. "Because that's sure as hell what it looked like."

"Would you quit saying hell? I taught you better."

She struggled with her anger. *I will not strangle him.* "Can you tell me what crony friend you rooked into helping with your little act of felony?"

He shrugged his shoulders. "Ernest owed me."

Oh, not sweet Ernest Burns. "Gramps, how could you?"

"He's on the board for the reenactment activities for the anniversary of the raid on Lawrence."

"That makes it okay to lie? Lie."

"How do you know if I'm lying or not?" His eyebrows rose in question.

Busted. She clamped her lips shut. She couldn't confess she'd been watching his browser history on her laptop.

"Sadie girl?"

"I think I need some time alone. I'm headed into town."

Chapter Fifteen

Judson found himself at odds. He shook his head as his thoughts reviewed what Walt had done for him this morning. Lying and cheating were two vices he hated. Not only had he not told the truth at the hospital, now he was party to another lie. Guilt gnawed at his insides.

A couple of hours ago, he'd come outside to clear his head. He'd fixed loose boards on the barn and finished the repairs on the corral. He found it easier to focus on what Walt and Sadie needed fixed around the farm than uncover answers to his predicament.

The afternoon sun beat down on him as he inspected some loose rungs on the corral. Sweat pooled on his lower back. He grimaced as he dragged his shirt over his head and hung it on the gate.

A slight breeze danced down his spine, alleviating some of his discomfort from the sun. Thirty minutes later he rotated his arm and gazed down the line of corral he'd repaired. The exercise had felt good, relieving the stiffness in his arm.

He startled at a nip to the back of his leg. He glanced down and chuckled. The midnight black horse, Sinatra, stared at him with soulful eyes. "Hey, buddy. You almost had a piece of my hide."

Sinatra backed up and fluttered his lips.

He chuckled. "Are you laughing at me?" His gaze fell to the rest of his intent audience. The paint, Skittles, nickered at him as if amused by the antics. Backfire and Twinkie lingered a few feet away curiously watching him. Horses had always been a major part of his life. Full-size ones anyway. She had informed him these miniatures were no different.

He couldn't think of a better answer to relieve stress than grooming a horse. He retreated into the barn and found a currycomb in the supplies. Once back outside he sat on the ground and whispered words to Sinatra to sooth and coax him to come closer.

Soon all the horses were crowded around him vying for his attention, nipping at each other. "Now, hang on. There's no reason to be greedy. You'll each get your turn."

The tension slid away from his body as he focused on one horse after another. His motions automatic as his thoughts drifted.

He'd prayed for peace a couple of nights ago. Had this been the Lord's answer? He did work in mysterious ways. But placing him in the future? He shook his head in bewilderment.

He glanced at the house a short distance away. Walt's words from earlier danced through his mind. Take advantage and live. How would he make money here? His skills were over one hundred fifty years old. He couldn't live here at the Winters' farm forever. Sooner or later he'd need to get out on his own and make his own way.

What did he find scarier? Lost in his own time? Or in the future?

****

Sadie had no destination in mind when she'd left the house. She'd just driven. Mid-morning she found herself parked outside the Lawrence library, staring at the building. What answers would she find inside, if any?

She wished she'd brought her own laptop as she sat down at one of the public computer stations. Removing her cell phone from her pocket, she silenced the ringer. She tapped a finger on the keyboard as she recalled the items Gramps had searched.

The subjects still made no sense. She called to mind Judson's conversation at the hospital. He'd been out of his head with desperation for the town. Maybe her research needed to focus on Quantrill's raid.

She hadn't studied the event since high school. After she read a few articles she leaned back and rubbed her eyes. The sleepless nights were catching up with her. What answers were the two trying to find?

She shook her head and moved on to her next search. Time travel. Thirty minutes later her head throbbed. Words she'd never considered like law of casualty, cause, effect, and time dilation swirled in her brain. And those were the few words she remembered. Did she understand what she had read? Heck no.

She rose, stretched and reached for her purse. Her head pounded behind her temples. A moment later she dug a pain reliever bottle from the depths of her purse. She shook two tablets out into her palm and glanced about for a fountain.

Consulting her watch, she groaned. More time had passed than she realized. If she didn't hurry, Gramps would find something to get into.

The librarian studied the titles of the books she piled on the counter. "Some heavy reading. We have an excellent book on wormholes. If you'd be interested in checking that one out as well."

She tilted her head. Wormholes, another subject she was clueless about. "Sure, why not."

On the drive home, she considered the books on the seat beside her. Would they help shed any light on the problem troubling Judson?

Her heart fluttered in frustration as she drove into the drive. She'd left Gramps too long to his own devices. She slammed on the brakes and cursed. The empty space where his Chevy sat mocked her. She groaned. He was out driving with his bum foot and without the supportive boot she'd wager.

She leaned her forehead against the steering wheel. Weariness at the situation consumed her. On a good day her grandfather wore her out. But throw in the mix an unknown like their guest and she found herself past the point of exhaustion.

A scary thought came to her and she leaned up. Did he get taken against his will? Now the police weren't investigating, had Judson forced him to drive him somewhere? She should never have left them alone. Grabbing her cell from her purse, she dialed his phone. If the call forwarded to voicemail she'd phone the police straight away.

She breathed a sigh of relief when he answered on the third ring.

"Sadie girl. How are you doing? We understand we upset you earlier. You take all the time you need. Everything is fine at the farm."

The old lying buzzard. Did he get coerced into saying that? Did he have him at gunpoint somewhere? After all, they didn't know much about him. Over the last few days she'd let her guard down. She hadn't felt threatened by him. How could she be so off base about someone?

"Sadie?"

Anger replaced her fear. "Gramps. I would love to believe you right now, but I'm sitting in front of the house staring at your empty parking space."

"Crap."

"You took the word right out of my mouth. Now tell me the truth, Gramps. Please tell me he hasn't kidnapped you or is holding you at gunpoint somewhere. Do I need to call the police?"

"What the hell. Have you lost your ever-loving mind? Why would you think something like that?"

She rolled her eyes. "What do you expect me to think? You've not given me any reason to trust him. Or you. You've kept so many secrets these last few days."

He sighed. "Listen, we are on our way back to the farm. Cool your jets and we'll see you in a few minutes."

The dial tone echoed in her ear a second before she realized he'd hung up. He wanted her to chill, did he? Fine. She made her way to the barn.

"Hey guys, who's up for a bath?" The nickers of consent were instantaneous as she entered. She smiled as she led each mini, one by one, into the enclosure set up for such an activity. "Who wants to go first?"

She'd completed Skittles's and Twinkie's baths and started on Backfire when she recognized the creak of the barn door. She took a deep calming breath. It was time for Gramps to face the music and spill his guts.

Turning, she opened her mouth to let him have a piece of her mind, but instead she observed Judson as he leaned against the barn wall a few feet away.

He straightened. "Can I lend a hand?"

He wore another polo she bought him and the shirt looked as good as the last. She nodded and turned back to her task. Why did her heart have to patter so?

They worked side by side in silence until they finished Backfire's bath.

"Sadie?"

She jumped at the unexpected intrusion of her thoughts. She glanced at him before tying Sinatra's halter to the post in the bathing area. "Yes?"

He wiped a smudge of dirt from her cheek. "You know I would never intentionally do anything to hurt Walt or you, right? I appreciate the kindness and support both of you have shown me."

She swallowed hard at the feel of his caress. This man did things to her nervous system she'd never experienced before. She looked into his eyes and searched for any deception lurking in the depths. Again, she was struck by the color. "Where did you convince Gramps to go today? Or is the destination a secret as well?"

He held his hands up in surrender. "He took me to a local place that makes wine. He wanted to pick up a bottle. His idea, not mine."

She turned away to wash Sinatra. Great. Gramps purchased alcohol he wasn't supposed to have. Again. She stopped scrubbing and admitted, "It's hard for me to trust. Especially when I feel I've been lied to."

A heavy sigh reverberated around the area. "I don't like deception either." He paused before he continued. "I don't belong here."

She turned and witnessed him rubbing the back of his neck in a nervous gesture. The question bouncing around in her brain for days emerged, "Were you shot because you were doing something illegal?"

"No." The answer burst forth, ringing with honesty.

"Then what? Why all the secrecy between you and Gramps?"

He took the sponge from her hands and stroked the horse. Suds emerged as he continued to rub in gentle strokes. "I've struggled with a problem the last few days and he has attempted to help me."

She placed a hand over his to still his actions. "You don't feel you can trust me?"

"It's not I don't have faith in you. I don't want you thinking I'm crazy."

Why should her thoughts be important to him? "I want to help, Judson. Please, let me."

Several emotions crossed his face before he nodded. "I'm not from here."

She didn't understand. "You've already said that."

Frustration radiated from his body. "I was born in the year eighteen thirty four."

She let his words sink in a moment. Gramps's search on time travel and choice of last night's movie now made sense. The expression on his face dared her to believe him. "How did you get here?"

His hand shook as he raked his fingers through his hair. "I don't know. One minute I rode toward Lawrence to warn the mayor of the city about Quantrill and the next I travelled in a square moving box on the way to a hospital."

Wait. Had he been shot by the guerrilla leader himself? "Who shot you?"

"Two of Quantrill's scouts, Les and Earl. They

jumped me on the outskirts of Eudora." He turned back toward Sinatra. "It's my fault all those men and boys perished the night of the raid."

Guilt plagued his words. She retreated to the other side of the horse. "How can you say that?"

"Don't you see? My responsibility was to warn Lawrence. Mine." He waved a hand at his surroundings. "I'm not worthy of the second chance Walt believes I deserve."

The conviction of his words gave her pause. Did she believe he travelled in time? Would the books she'd brought home from the library hold answers? Could they find in the literature a reasonable explanation for the situation he found himself in?

Wait. According to his story the raid already happened. Which took place on the twenty-first of August. Today was the eighteenth. Would it be possible to transport him back to his own time on the twenty-first? "Let's finish Sinatra's bath and then I will show you the books I checked out from the library. Between the three of us maybe we can figure out what happened."

Chapter Sixteen

Her vision blurred as she scanned the last chapter of the book she held. She leaned her head back against the couch before her gaze roamed to the other occupants in the room. Gramps reclined in his chair, his supportive boot back on his foot, and Judson leaned on the other couch arm. They'd looked through the reading materials she'd brought home for a couple of hours. She'd caught a little bit of grief from Gramps after she explained how she knew what information to check out from the library. He'd not been happy to find out she'd been spying on his Internet use.

"Anyone find anything useful?"

Judson's gaze met hers, his confusion as obvious as her own. "My schoolin' didn't prepare me for these type of facts."

Walt grunted and didn't glance up from his reading.

Laying aside the book she held, she rose. "I need to take a break. I'll go start dinner."

"Wait." Gramps had put down his recliner's footrest and wore an excited expression upon his face. He waved the hardback in the air. "Wormholes. What if he travelled through one of those?"

She sat back down and frowned. "I thought those were only in space."

"Space?" Judson leaned forward, intent to learn

something new.

Now she understood his childlike interest in the movie the night before. The things common in her world hadn't existed in his. She smiled, ready to blow his mind. "We've had ships and machines travel into outer space. Men have landed on the moon."

Walt waved a hand. "Never mind the history lesson now, you can tell him later. I think I'm onto something." He tapped a finger to his chin. "Tomorrow the Watkins Museum has tours retracing Quantrill's route of his raid."

She shook her head. Where was he going with this conversation? "Are you wanting to take him on the tour?"

"Exactly."

She shook her head and frowned in confusion. "Why? I guess I don't comprehend the point."

He grunted again. "If we hike the path, maybe we can find where he appeared and then determine a way for him to get back to his time through a wormhole, like this book describes."

What he explained made sense. But in truth, she didn't know if the book he held was fiction or nonfiction.

"It's worth the gamble." Judson stood and paced to the window. "I need to know if I have the chance to warn the people. To make my mistake right."

She couldn't understand the struggle the man before her faced. She did appreciate his honor and conviction though. "Gramps, I need to study what you're reading. But I need some pain reliever and food in my stomach first."

Judson watched as she left the room. He found

himself torn between his duty as a soldier and of a man. She had listened to his story and insisted on helping. Not once did she laugh at his or Walt's foolishness about time travel. Doubt had to trouble her like it did him, but she hadn't voiced aloud any disbelief in him or his story. Another problem he faced was his mounting affection for her and the knowledge he would leave her behind.

Chapter Seventeen

A knock at her kitchen door later in the evening startled her. She finished washing the dish she held before she dried her hands. Who could be at their back door this time of night?

She flipped the yard light on and took a quick peek out the window. Seriously? Twice in one week? Troy stood in the dim light swatting a bug.

Why did she have to switch the light on? Now he knew she had seen him. She unlocked the door and swung it open.

A smooth smile graced his lips. "Evenin' Sadie."

"Troy." He stared at her without a word. The silence felt awkward. Frustrated, she broke the quiet. "What are you doing here?"

He shrugged his shoulders. "I don't know why I'm here." He stared down at his feet and shuffled them. "Tracy and I had a fight."

She leaned against the doorjamb and sighed. "I'm sorry to hear you're having problems, but shouldn't you talk to her and work through things with her? If she finds out you were here, it will add to your dilemma."

He glanced out into the night. "You're right." His gaze swung back to meet hers. "After I saw you at the mall, I've wondered if I've made a mistake."

Her stomach lurched. The last couple of months she'd suffered pure hell and he had the nerve to stand in front of her to say he made a mistake. About them? She didn't want to ask, but found the words emerging from her lips anyway. "About what?"

A sad smile appeared upon his lips. "Us."

She forced down the urge to groan. Why did she ask? Had he ever pulled this stunt on Tracy? She marveled at the nerve of the man.

"Can I come in?"

Don't be stupid. Don't be stupid. Her mind raced. "It's late. Go home, Troy."

He stepped forward, reached out and caressed her cheek. "I want to talk."

A few short months ago his caress would have made her heart flutter. But tonight…nothing. A good sign.

"Sadie asked you to leave."

She jerked at the quiet voice from behind. She observed Judson leaning against the kitchen doorframe, no shirt, denims low on his hips, and arms crossed. The white bandage over his wound stood out in stark contrast against his chest in the dim light.

"Who the hell are you?"

She groaned as Troy stepped past her into the kitchen. The amount of testosterone bouncing about the room made her cringe.

"Judson Stone. And you are?"

"Troy Lewis. Sadie's boyfriend."

She grabbed his forearm. "Ex." She glared at him. "You lost the boyfriend status when you became engaged to Tracy. Go home to your fiancée."

He ran a hand through his hair. "I can't. She broke our engagement tonight."

His words smacked her in the face. He didn't have

a change of heart about their relationship; he didn't want to be alone. "I'm sorry, Troy, but you need to go home and work things out."

He pointed an accusing finger toward Judson. "Is he the one you bought the boxers for? Is he living here?"

Where did he get off using that accusatory tone? Astonishment whirled in her brain.

Judson straightened and crossed the tile floor. "Go on to bed, Sadie. I'll lock up."

She suppressed a giggle. The expression of shock on Troy's face was priceless. He'd jumped to the conclusion she was sleeping with Judson. It served him right. The imp inside of her danced to life as she leaned up and gave Judson a quick kiss on his cheek. "Don't be too long."

He stared at her retreating back. She glanced over her shoulder and he was surprised to see her silent laughter in her gaze. The jolt of awareness he'd felt at the graze of her lips on his cheek had surprised him. The other man had put him on edge. He wasn't unhappy Troy had misunderstood his words. He hoped he hadn't angered her. But if her glance held any indication, she'd been amused.

His gaze swung back to the other man. He shifted on his bare feet and gestured a hand toward the door. "I'm locking up now." Satisfaction swept down his spine as his nostrils flared in irritation before Troy swiveled and stalked out into the night.

He stepped out on the porch. The warm night breeze caressed his bare chest. The uninvited man's door slammed shut before his metal beast sped from the yard. The annoyance he had felt when he had spied him at the door surprised him. Had he ever felt such resentment so quickly against another human? He rubbed a hand across his face. The feisty female who resided in the house twisted him in knots. His cheek still tingled from where she'd placed her innocent kiss. The night noises faded as his thoughts turned to his angel. He realized she wasn't, like he'd first imagined. But in his mind she'd always be one.

Returning to the kitchen, he locked the door behind him. As he doused the lights she called out to him. He paused in her bedroom doorway. She sat cross-legged on her bed still fully dressed. His stomach quivered in response to the smile she bestowed.

"Do you need help changing your bandage?"

He shrugged. "I believe I can manage."

She nodded as if her mind were elsewhere. Had he made a mistake by stepping in to help? Did she want to be with Troy? "I'm sorry if I overstepped."

Her gaze shot up to meet his. "No. I'm sorry." She waved her hands. "I should have handled the situation on my own. He'd taken my silence for consent, instead of shock."

Should he ask what happened in their relationship?

She gave a small smile. "Did you see his face? Priceless. He believes we're sleeping together."

The image and desire erupting in his head at her words had him taking a step back. Inside his head the idea wasn't such a laughing matter. "It's late and I'm tired. Sounds like Walt has a big day planned tomorrow. I'll say good night."

The sparkle in her gaze disappeared. "Good night." She rose from the bed. "Oh, I left your medicine on the bathroom counter. Don't forget to take your last dose for the day."

"All right. Thanks."

Chapter Eighteen

The first fingers of dawn infiltrated her curtains as she awoke. She leaned up on her elbow to check the time. The numbers glared back and indicated she had a few minutes before the alarm sounded. She yawned. Sleep had almost been nonexistent again last night. She'd tossed and turned. Her brain hadn't shut down. Thoughts of Gramp's dishonesty, Judson's situation, wormholes and Troy's visit danced through her mind.

She sat up and stared at the floor. Each problem plagued her last night and she didn't doze off until almost dawn. The most unnerving riddle in her brain was the lengths her grandfather took to get the heat from the police off Judson. She rubbed at her eyes. His belief in his story amazed her. Why couldn't she be as trusting?

The echo of her alarm clock in the room's silence made her groan. Another day beckoned and sitting here wool gathering didn't solve anything. She made quick work of showering and about twenty minutes later set to the task of feeding the horses.

****

The house seemed quiet as Judson made his way into the kitchen. The last few days Sadie made breakfast by this time. The lights were on, but the room appeared unoccupied.

The smell of coffee filled the air. Someone had

already brewed a pot. He ambled over to retrieve a cup. The machine fascinated him. Walt had showed him how it worked yesterday while she'd been in town. He leaned over and inhaled the fragrance.

"Good morning, son."

He jumped. He hadn't heard his approach.

A hand settled on his shoulder. "Sorry, I didn't mean to startle you."

He cradled the empty coffee cup. "I'm enjoying the aroma. Thanks for putting some on."

He shook his head. "I didn't. Sadie must have made the pot. Have you seen her this morning?"

He poured a cup and sat down at the table. "Not yet."

"Maybe she's out in the barn."

She had her hands full. Not only did she take care of her grandfather, but she handled the horses and a job outside the home. She didn't need him to add to her burdens. "Walt, do you think there's a way for me to go back to where I belong?"

"I'm not sure, but who says you couldn't belong here?"

He held up a hand to stop him. "I know you meant well by telling the officer the story you did, but the truth is gnawing at my insides. I hope we can find some answers today. I need to finish my mission."

"I'm not sure what to expect today, but I don't think you can change the past, son."

He rose from his chair in frustration. "How do you know? Who's to say I changed history. All I know is I'm here safe and I didn't complete my mission." He ran a hand through his hair. "Lives were lost because of me."

He scratched his chin and pondered his question. "You're right. I don't know. Maybe you've already done the changing by your presence here." He leaned over and unfastened the Velcro straps on the boot covering his sprained ankle. "You can't take the blame for everything that occurred. You need to let go of the guilt."

"Gramps, what are you doing?"

Judson's gaze met hers. How long had she stood in the kitchen doorway?

He harrumphed. "What does it look like? I'm going to drive Judson into town."

She rolled her eyes and made her way to the coffee pot. "I don't think so." After she poured a cup she turned and sipped. "You don't mind if I tag along, do you?" She slipped the set of keys on the table into her hand. "I'm driving, by the way."

"What about your trip into town to the assisted living center?"

He noted how tired she appeared. Had his situation put the shadows under her eyes or had Troy caused her unrest?

"I've left a message I'll be at the center this afternoon. I didn't think our mission would take the full day." Her gaze met his own after a few seconds. "You don't mind if I tag along, do you?"

He shook his head. "I appreciate the help. From both of you."

The speed in which they travelled still amazed him. He stared out the truck's window at the farms and fields they passed. He imagined where he'd been ambushed the other night. Had the location been close to the Winters' farm?

As if reading his thoughts, she asked, "Where were you when you got shot the other night?"

"I'd ridden past the settlement of Hesper and neared Eudora when I got ambushed by Les and Earl."

Walt leaned up from the back seat. "There isn't much left of Hesper." He scratched his chin. "I don't believe you were too far from our farm. Do you remember where the ambulance picked you up?"

He closed his eyes and recalled the night of his arrival. When he'd regained consciousness, he'd found himself strapped inside the traveling box. He shook his head in frustration. "No. I have no idea where they found me."

She offered him a soft smile. "We will see if we can get some answers at the Watkins Museum. They should have a map of Quantrill's route. The information we gather from them will give us a better clue of where you got hurt."

A couple of hours later, Judson's stomach churned in revulsion. He fought the bile that rose in his throat. The details from the raid were gruesome. Visiting the museum had made him feel worse. Could he have made a difference if he'd arrived in time? He wasn't sure. Why had Les and Earl wounded him instead of killing him outright? None of the details made sense.

She placed a hand on his arm. "Are you okay?"

He shook his head and his gaze met hers. "No." His voice cracked as the one word wrenched from his body.

Walt cleared his throat and placed a hand on his arm. "I can't begin to understand what you feel or what you are going through. Do you want to drive back to the house? We don't have to continue our search for answers today."

He shook his head. "We'll run out of time. The raid takes place in a couple of days, in my time anyway. I need to see this through. Where had you planned to go next?"

Walt studied the map in his hand. "Let's begin at the Miller House."

Chapter Nineteen

Sadie methodically prepared Backfire and Twinkie for their visit to the Cedar Ridge Assisted Living Center. The morning's activities weighed heavy on her mind. Judson rode in silence as they drove back from town earlier. He had good reason to be upset. Did he believe he could have stopped what happened in Lawrence?

After the Museum, they'd driven the route of Quantrill's raid and concluded in the end the location of Judson's ambush occurred outside of town closer to their farm. Could there be a wormhole near their house? The possibility astounded her. She frowned. She still had a problem believing the theory, especially here in Kansas.

"Can I help?"

A startled squeal escaped her lips and her hand flew to her chest. She turned to find Judson observing her. "You know it's not polite to sneak up on a person."

A sheepish expression appeared upon his face. "Sorry. I thought you heard me come in."

"Well, I didn't." She shook off her fright and handed Backfire's reins to him. "Since you're here you can help me load them into the trailer."

He tilted his head. "Where are you taking them?"

She scanned his features. He didn't seem as tense as earlier when they'd come home from their research

115

trip. "Remember when I told you I've been training the horses for therapy reasons?" He nodded his head in the affirmative. "Well, once a month we visit the elderly in town who live at the Cedar Ridge Assisted Living Center. We spend time with the residents and they get to pet, comb and cuddle these little cuties." She scratched behind Twinkie's ear. "I think the horses enjoy the visit as much as the residents."

"Does Walt accompany you?"

"Not always. Most of the time I go on my own." She packed the currycombs and other supplies before she cast a glance his way. "You're more than welcome to come along."

"I'd love to, if you don't mind."

She could tell from his expression he searched for an excuse to take his mind off his dilemma and what he'd learned. "I'd love the help."

A few minutes later the horses were secured, and she waited for him to settle into the passenger seat. He clicked his safety belt. "The strap doesn't rub against your wound, does it?"

He shook his head. "No. It's fine."

She grabbed the key in the ignition and started the truck. "Alrighty, then…we'll head out." She adjusted the air conditioner dial before she sneaked another peek at him. "Let me know if you get cold."

"The air feels wonderful." He cleared his throat. "Your modern conveniences amaze me. I love the glass box in the bathroom the best."

She laughed at his expression of awe on his face. "Yeah, I'd be pretty lost without the shower."

His gaze danced with amusement as their gazes met.

"You know, now I'm privy to your secret you've protected, could you tell me a little bit more about yourself?"

"I'm glad you know my situation. I realize we should have told you sooner." He shrugged his shoulders. "What do you want to know?"

She tapped her fingers against the wheel. "I don't know. Tell me about your life in eighteen sixty-three."

He glanced out the truck window a moment before his gaze swung back to her own. The sadness reflected in his gaze made her heart ache. "I guess I could describe my life as hard. I'd become embittered with the war."

She swallowed the lump in her throat. "I can't even imagine."

He shook his head as if to dislodge an image from his mind. "Tell me, Sadie. Are times better? Here? Now?"

She fought a wave of sadness threatening to consume her. "In some ways, yes. But we still have war if that's what you're asking."

He sighed and closed his eyes. "I prayed for peace, the other night on my ride to Lawrence."

She knew better than to ask if he'd found the tranquility he sought. Their visit to the museum earlier had taken care of any peace of mind he may have found. She struggled to think of a topic to lighten the mood and felt relief when a few moments later they arrived at the center. "We're here." She patted his jean-clad thigh. "You can tell me later about your antics as a young boy."

A rusty laugh escaped his lips. "What makes you think I have any stories to relate?"

She shook her head. "You're too much like Gramps. Trust me, there are stories." The keys jingled as she dragged them from the ignition. "Come on. Help me unload the crew."

Another chuckle escaped from him as he exited the truck.

She enjoyed hearing his laughter. Backfire and Twinkie greeted her with soft nickers as she opened the trailer door. "Oh, by the way, the reason Walt doesn't usually accompany me to the center is because of the pinchers."

A frown marred his brow. "I don't understand."

She snickered. "I know. But oh, you will."

Sandy Rogers, the director of the facility met them at the entrance and held the door open for them. "Good afternoon, Sadie." She ran a hand over Twinkie's and Backfire's coats as they passed by. "It's good to see you guys too."

"Hi, Sandy."

"Walt didn't accompany you today?"

They stopped at the front desk. "Gramps has had a little excitement this week. He twisted his ankle." She introduced him. "Meet Judson Stone. He is my helper for the day."

"Ma'am."

The older woman smiled at him and held out her hand. "Nice to meet you." She turned back to address her. "I'm sorry to hear Walt hurt himself. Tell him I hope he bounces back soon."

She chuckled. "You know Gramps. Not much keeps him down for long."

"True."

She ran her fingers through Backfire's mane. "I'm

sorry we couldn't come in earlier, but we helped Judson run some errands."

Sandy placed a hand on her arm. "That's fine. I'm glad you were able to come. We have a new resident I would like for you and the horses to meet."

Concern lined the other woman's face. "What seems to be the problem?" Now she wished she'd brought Skittles. She could win a crowd over in mere moments.

Sandy wrung her hands. "I'm not sure. Lucille acts like she wants to participate, but in the end...doesn't."

"Hmmm." She glanced down at Backfire. "I think we have our work cut out for us today, buddy. Are you ready to go entertain the troops?" The mini stared up at her with a soulful look. She chuckled before she made her way down the hall to the entertainment area.

Several voices called out a few moments later once they were spotted. "Hey, Sadie the horse lady is here. Where's Walt? Who's the stud muffin accompanying you?"

She smiled and held up a hand. "One at a time, please. First, did you miss me and my critters?" She waited until everyone quieted down before she made her way toward the new resident Sandy had pointed out. The older woman looked classy. Not a silver hair on her head out of place. She held out a hand. "I don't believe we've met. I'm Sadie Winters."

Lucille blinked her pale blue eyes but didn't utter a word or return the greeting.

He cleared his throat and his baritone voice broke the silence. "Good afternoon, ma'am. My name is Judson Stone."

The older lady's gaze shifted to her companion. A

flicker of emotion mirrored a brief moment in her gaze before it disappeared.

She brought Backfire closer to her chair. "This little guy is Backfire." People always asked about his name, but the horse chose the moment to let loose a bit of his namesake. A blush warmed her cheeks. "Well, now you know how he got his name."

The lady's demeanor changed in an instant. Her vacant glassy expression disappeared. First, a smile appeared on her face, then a deep belly laugh emerged.

A moment ticked by before she got her laughter under control. "Oh, my dear, you made my day." She withdrew a hanky from her pocket and wiped a tear from her eye.

She tilted her head. "I did?"

"Absolutely. Not only did you bring this handsome young man along who reminds me of my late husband, but you also brought along your mini horse who sounds and expels like my late husband." She dabbed at another tear. "Thank you. I'm Lucille Smith, by the way."

The occupants who heard the exchange joined Lucille in her laughter. She smiled and gave Backfire an approving pet.

A few hours later she waved a hand to the residents and led Backfire away from his admirers.

"I'm happy with today's visit. A good day indeed." She smiled at Judson as he opened the trailer door.

He studied her a moment. "What you and your horses are trained to do is a good thing. The cheer these two little guys brought today to those elderly amazed me."

Pride filled her at his words. She nibbled on her

lower lip. "I'm glad the challenging work has started to pay off. I've worked hard to get this venture off the ground. Nothing makes me feel better than the joy I bring to people, whether it's for an hour or two. My goal is to quit my day job and provide therapy full time." She shrugged her shoulders. "That's the hope anyway."

"I know the people you visited today appreciated the visit."

She giggled. "And you too…stud muffin."

He frowned. "What do those words mean?"

A frown wrinkled his brow as if trying to understand her words. "Let's say the residents felt you were praiseworthy eye candy." His bewilderment didn't ease. She giggled and winked. "What the term means is they think you are nice to gawk at."

He groaned. "That's not all they felt I was worthy of. I lost track of how many times my backside got pinched. I'm not sure which is worse, a switch to my hide, or the residents of Cedar Ridge Assisted Living Center. I'm going to be black and blue by tomorrow."

Laughter bubbled out as he rubbed at said offended area. "Now you know why Walt tries to limit his visits."

A jaunty tune from her cell phone interrupted their merriment. She smiled as she answered her best friend Jess's call. "Hey there."

"Want to get out of the house tonight?"

She chuckled, tucked the phone between her shoulder and ear before she closed the door on the trailer "You betcha booty I would. Where do you want to meet?"

She finished her call and replaced her cell in her

pocket. She glanced at him and noticed a bewildered expression upon his face. "What's wrong?"

He shook his head and took a step back. "Uh, nothing."

Well, okay. "You're doubtless ready to relax. Let's head home."

Chapter Twenty

Silence filled the truck cab as they drove back to the farm. She bit her lip as she cast a glance at him. His quiet was an eerie weight in the small space. What had happened back at the center? They'd had a good time until she received the call from Jess.

Gramps met them in the kitchen as they entered through the back door. "How did the horses' visit go?"

"Oh Gramps. You should've been at the center today. Backfire did a wonderful job of breaking the ice for a new resident." She took a moment to tell him about the mini's afternoon.

"Oh sweetie. That's great. The hard work you've put in has started to pay off."

A wave of pride spread through her body. Her plan with the therapy horses was coming together.

"Not to change the subject, but I thought I had better let you know Rita will be over tonight to visit me."

She cringed privately in her mind. The infamous Rita. The reason for his lame duck situation. Should she be leery? "Is she the reason you felt the need to leave yesterday and go purchase a bottle of wine? Should I be worried about the leaded drinks planned for the evening?"

He crossed his heart and grinned. "I promise. I will not over indulge. No shenanigans this time...of that nature."

The old smoothie. Rita didn't stand a chance with this heart breaker. "I don't have bail money saved up. Keep that little tidbit in mind."

He gave a brief salute. "Aye, aye, Captain." He winked. "What are your plans this evening?"

"Jess asked me to dinner."

Judson leaned against the kitchen counter. "You're not meeting Troy?"

"Troy." Gramps bellowed. "Why would she have plans with him, the no-good bum?"

She squirmed under the scrutiny of two sets of inquiring gazes. "He stopped by last night after you had gone to bed."

"What did he want?" He held up a hand. "Never mind. I know what the no good wanted." He exited the room grumbling under his breath.

She turned on Judson. "Why did you bring up Troy in front of Gramps?" He shrugged his shoulders but didn't comment. "Listen, I appreciated the help last night, but let me handle telling Gramps my problems."

She spun on her heel and left the room. Her agitation evident in each step she took. He ran a hand through his hair and rubbed his neck. He hadn't handled the situation well. He wanted to know if the person she spoke to in the small square box was Troy.

He paced a few feet and stared out the kitchen window. Now the name Jess agitated him instead. How many men courted her? What were these emotions that ran rampant throughout his body? His thoughts had focused on the war for so long he didn't know how to handle any type of relationship with a woman. He enjoyed her company. Her inner and outer beauty often caught him off guard. How do you go about wooing a woman in this time?

"Why didn't you tell me about Troy earlier?"

Startled from his reverie, he turned and met Walt's gaze. "Wasn't my place."

"Hmmpf. And it is now?"

He rotated his neck to ease the tension in his muscles. "Walt, look. I don't know why I brought Troy up."

A few seconds passed before a smile settled on his lips. "I think I do, son. I've seen the signs before."

He frowned, bewildered at what he meant. "I don't understand what you're saying."

"There's a gleam in your eye whenever Sadie enters the room."

"Walt, you don't know what I think. How could you? Everything is new and unfamiliar to me."

He placed a hand on his shoulder. "I know you're confused, son. But I know when someone is smitten. I think you suffer from a small bite of the jealousy bug."

He shook his head. Could he be jealous? He didn't have much experience with the reaction. Did that explain his ailment? "Could be. I'm not sure. My focus has been about staying alive for so long, I'd forgotten there are other emotions besides anger and sadness."

Walt glanced out the window. "My date is here. Go and talk to her before she goes to meet Jess."

"Walt."

He paused at the kitchen door. "Yes?"

"Is her relationship with Jess serious?"

He could swear a twinkle appeared in the older man's gaze. "Totally."

Chapter Twenty-One

She eyed the sundress she'd chosen in the mirror. What she wore to meet Jess shouldn't have mattered, so why had she spent the last hour rejecting one outfit after another? Her disgusted gaze landed on the discarded pile of clothes on her bed. Primping wasn't her style.

Let's face it. She wasn't trying to dress her best for Jess, but for the guest Gramps had invited into their home. She studied her reflection one last time before she left her bedroom.

She paused in the hall. A woman's laugh greeted her ears. Gramps' friend had arrived while she'd been in her room deciding what to wear. She smoothed down her dress and entered the living room. Gramps sat in his recliner like a king who entertained on his throne. A lovely petite older woman sat on the couch next to Judson.

"Gramps, I'm heading out." She turned and stuck out her hand. "You must be Rita. It's a pleasure to meet you."

The older woman laughed. "Oh, I don't know. I'm part of the reason you have this invalid on your hands."

Her laughter joined Rita's. "True, but you are the one doing me a favor by babysitting the old codger tonight."

"Hey. I'm right here."

They continued to laugh as he frowned. She leaned

over and gave him a kiss on his forehead. "Don't wait up."

"Try to behave."

Her gaze met Judson's. When she'd entered the room, he'd risen from the couch. She flashed a smile at him. "Now where is the fun in that?"

His gaze followed her from the room as her laughter trailed off. She'd taken his breath away. Gone were the denims and faded shirts she'd worn the last couple of days. They'd been replaced by a short, bright red dress and her lip color matched. He swallowed hard and shifted his feet. His thoughts turned to the curves and skin he'd glimpsed. The clinging material emphasized her breasts, her bare shoulders and the hem didn't touch her knees. He glanced at Walt. He didn't seem to be fazed by his granddaughter's outfit. Why would he let her leave the house dressed as such? And why did he care so much?

He ran a hand through his hair. A wave of envy washed over him as he thought how lucky Jess was tonight to enjoy her company. He pivoted and announced over his shoulder, "I'll go check on the horses."

****

Her friend Jessica Sage waited outside for her as she parked at their favorite Mexican restaurant.

She fanned herself. "Why didn't you go in? The temperature is sweltering out here."

Her friend smiled. "I had just arrived when I saw you pull up. So, I thought I would wait. Love your dress, by the way. What's the occasion?" She squinted at her. "Are you blushing?"

She grabbed her friend's arm and opened the door.

"It's got to be the heat. Let's go inside and cool off."

As they were seated Jess leaned over and whispered, "Spill. What's up at the Winters' farm?"

She squirmed in the booth. Did she have an answer to her question? She smiled at her best friend since first grade. "Why do you think something's up?"

She sniffed the air. "Because I smell trouble brewing."

She wound her napkin in her lap. "You know Gramps twisted his ankle the other day."

"Yes, I know." She tilted her head. "But that isn't what is eating at you."

"Well, I have more than one invalid at the house at the moment." Her friend tilted her head, a frown upon her brow.

"I don't understand."

After she took a few moments to explain, her expression turned incredulous.

"Is Walt crazy? "

"I know, right?" She shrugged her shoulders. Even though she knew Judson's secret, she still didn't understand her grandfather's actions. "Thank you for suggesting dinner tonight. I needed the break."

Her friend studied her with keen interest.

She glanced down at her dress. Did she have some salsa on her outfit? "What?"

She tapped a finger on her lips. "Oh, I don't know. I'm wondering what this Judson fellow looks like."

She hoped the heat that rose on her cheeks didn't give her away.

"Ah ha. As I suspected. You like him, don't you?"

Before she could answer, someone cleared their throat.

"Jessica. Sadie. How are you this evening?"

Again? Mentally she rolled her eyes. Was he stalking her? Her gaze met his. "What a surprise, Troy." Her mild sarcasm didn't faze him as he shrugged his shoulders.

"I was out with friends and thought I spotted you."

She gazed about the room. Tracy didn't seem to be present.

He caught her look. "Oh, I told them to go on ahead and I'd catch up." He pointed to the booth. "Mind if I sit down for a minute?"

On the verge of saying yes, he scooted onto the bench, crowding into her space. *Well, okay. Go ahead and make yourself comfortable.*

"I wanted to apologize for last night."

She caught Jess's quirked brow. That conversation hadn't come up. Yet. "Troy."

He placed a hand on her bare arm. "No, wait. Hear me out." He glanced at Jess before he continued. "Can I talk to you privately?"

She lifted his hand from her arm. "What you have to say can be said in front of Jess."

"When I saw you at the store the other day I realized how much I'd missed you."

Unbelievable. "What about Tracy? Your fiancée? You can't have both of us."

"I told you. She broke our engagement last night once she realized I still had feelings for you."

Anger bubbled just below the surface. He'd messed with her mind the last few days. Had he always been this conniving? He probably hadn't broken his engagement off. She took a sip from her water glass. The chilled liquid didn't cool her anger. She gritted her teeth in an attempt to keep calm. "I'm not available, Troy."

An expression of shock stole over his face before being replaced with disbelief. "You can't be talking about the stranger at your house."

She tilted her head and studied him. How did he know Judson was a stranger? Someone had snooped. She shrugged her shoulders. "Why does who I invite into my home matter to you? You and I are not together."

He stood suddenly. "I know you brought a stranger home from the hospital." He slapped a hand against his thigh. "He isn't a stray puppy, Sadie. You know nothing about him."

She wiped her mouth with her napkin and counted to ten. "Troy. The fact I have a guest in my home is no concern of yours." She pointed a finger at him then back at herself. "We aren't a couple anymore. Have you forgotten? Besides, consider how well I thought I knew you and see how that fiasco ended."

He released a huff. "I'm not giving up on us."

She sighed and kept an eye on him until he exited the restaurant. He could get a gold medal for his persistence. "I think I need a stronger drink than water."

Jess laughed and signaled their waiter. "I think I agree."

Chapter Twenty-Two

Judson lay awake in bed and stared at the shadows that danced on the ceiling. Not wanting to interfere with Walt's date, he'd spent most of the night in the barn. He'd whittled and talked through his problems with the horses.

His gaze landed on the timepiece on the wall. Rita had left over an hour ago, according to the clock. Now midnight approached. He relaxed his hands when he realized they were clenched into fists. When had he last worried this much? He sat up in bed and ran his hands through his hair. Damn it. She'd stepped out with another man. He'd let that thought burn a hole in his stomach the whole evening and the idea left him unsettled.

What Walt said rang true. Jealousy ate at his gut. He didn't like the sensation. Not one bit.

His ears perked as a sound registered with him. The noise came from just outside. Either an intruder made the racket, or she'd come home. He grabbed his discarded denims and slipped into them before he padded barefoot down the hall to the kitchen. Pausing in the doorway, he stared at a tall blonde helping Sadie through the door.

She giggled and put a finger to her mouth. "Shhh. You'll wake everyone."

The other woman laughed. "I know, but you're the

noisy one."

Her gaze snagged his. "Oops. Too late. Busted."

The other woman's gaze landed on him. "You must be Judson." At his nod, she held out a hand. "I'm Jess. It's a pleasure to meet you."

Shock and relief rippled down his spine. Jess was a woman? The thought had never entered his mind. The tight knot in his gut eased. "Good to meet you as well." He tilted his head. "What's going on?"

She stumbled as Sadie leaned against her. "Well, our buddy here decided she needed a drink. Or two." She stopped and appeared deep in thought. "Now that I think about it, she may have had three."

He frowned. Did his ears deceive him? He shook his head. She did appear to be drunk.

She slipped out from under her arm and sat down hard in a kitchen chair. "I'm tired."

Jess patted her on the shoulder. "You've had a difficult week. Get some rest. I need to get home. I'm surprised David hasn't sent a search party out for me."

She rested her head on her folded arms on the table. "Thanks, Jess. I had fun. Good night."

"Me too. Will you try to make church tomorrow?"

"Mmmm."

"I'll take your answer as a maybe. I'll have your truck at church for you to bring home, just in case." She turned and eyed him. "Nice to meet you. Night."

He stood and stared at the back door a minute before he focused on her. "Do you need help?"

She groaned and peeked at him from under her bangs. "Yup."

He smiled as he realized she even looked beautiful mussed. Leaning forward he placed a hand under her arm. "Careful now." She stumbled slightly as she stood.

She leaned into his chest. "I feel like I'm on a Tilt o' Whirl."

She burrowed into his neck. Her breath caressed his skin as she sighed. Every single one of her curves pressed to his frame. Heart pounding, he breathed in the fragrance clinging to her short tresses. His angel smelled and felt wonderful in his arms.

Her pert nose nuzzled his neck. "Mmm…you smell nice."

She'd read his thoughts. His body responded as she snuggled closer. Temptation had never been so appealing. "Sadie." He groaned as she slipped her arms around his neck and her lips travelled upward to nip at his ear. "Let me help you to your room."

She leaned back and smiled. "Or your room? I'm not picky."

The friskiness was the liquor talking. But his body overruled his conscience. Her blue gaze sparkled in drunken mischief. His gaze dropped to her lips as her tongue darted out to lick her bottom one. He listened to the voice of reason inside his head, but desire flared and he wanted to shout to hell with it. He shouldn't take advantage. She wasn't herself.

"What is wrong with one itty bitty kiss?"

Everything his mind screamed. Nothing, his opposing enemy, his body, yelled. He inched closer and gazed upon her pouty lips before he leaned in to graze them in a tentative caress. Capturing the sigh that escaped, he deepened the kiss.

The blood pumping through his veins flowed like pure molten heat. Had he ever felt so alive? His pulse accelerated as he wrapped her tighter within his arms.

Moments later he raised his head to study her upturned face. Her eyes were closed, and her lips quivered. He backed her up, lifted and placed her upon the kitchen counter. A moan rent the air as her dress hiked up as his hands grazed her thighs. Had the sound come from him?

As if in a trance he stroked her exposed skin. So soft. He moved forward to settle his frame between her legs. A nibble to her neck brought forth a groan from her. His body shook as she locked her legs around his hips. An explosion from a stick of dynamite couldn't compare to the emotions erupting in his body. He growled as a shudder wracked her body. He took possession once again of her lips.

Suddenly she broke the connection and their gazes met. Could she hear or feel his heartbeat drum within his chest against her own? He blinked once, twice as she unhooked her legs from about his waist. He backed away. What had he been thinking? He hadn't been.

His hand shook as he ran his fingers through his short locks. "Sadie." Startled at his husky voice he cleared his throat and tried again. "I'm sorry. I didn't act properly."

She blinked owlishly at him before a giggle escaped. She put one hand to her mouth as the other smoothed her dress down before she scooted off her perch.

"I, uh…Good night, Judson."

He took a deep breath to calm his racing heart. He needed air. Easing open the door, he inhaled deeply. The night air still hung heavy with humidity. He leaned against the porch railing and closed his eyes. The frogs croaked by the creek and the cicadas' song filtered into his mind. Both calmed his raging body and thoughts. He opened his eyes to stare at the night sky. A shooting star streamed across the darkness. A tranquility he hadn't felt for some time filled his soul.

She floated down the hallway as if in a dream. She shut her door and slumped against it. *Holy Crap. What had just happened?* Goosebumps raced up her arms. She rubbed at them as she fought to ease the sensation. Had her world ever spun so out of control?

She'd love to blame the potency of the liquor, but his kiss unsettled her. Her body throbbed and hummed in an unfamiliar way. Troy had never made her feel this way. This queasy sensation came from a single kiss.

She recalled his uttered words of not acting proper. Hell, she'd take improper any day of the week if he dished it out. Every single nerve ending within her body danced as if they were alive. On trembling legs, she made her way to her bathroom.

She noted her swollen lips as she stared into the mirror. She touched them. The sparks she'd experienced in the kitchen replayed in her mind. Heat filled her cheeks at the loss of inhibition she'd displayed. What must he think of her?

Hours later she groaned and flung the sheet off her fevered body. Nothing good came from overindulging in tequila and getting revved up by a hot guy. The buzz from the margaritas had worn off hours ago. The effect from his kiss, not so much. She turned her head and studied her clock's digital read out. Three a.m.

Sleep wasn't coming anytime soon. She dragged a hand through her hair and swung her legs over the side of the bed. She glanced at the stack of books from the library on her dresser. They'd pretty much exhausted the contents and she wasn't sure she'd find any further useful information inside.

She retrieved her laptop instead. Twenty minutes later she stared in wonder at a photo she'd located of the Eleventh Kansas Cavalry. The image appeared grainy, but there was no doubt in her mind she stared at a photo of Judson. She leaned forward and squinted to examine the picture.

He wore a costume similar to what he'd arrived in at the emergency room. The screen blurred as she stifled a yawn. She shut her computer and nibbled her lower lip. The last finger of doubt vanished in her mind. He had travelled in time and they needed to help him get back. Even though she didn't want him to go.

Chapter Twenty-Three

Alone at the kitchen table early the next morning, she cradled her head and groaned as the sound of the coffee maker dripping reverberated through her skull. The deprivation of sleep and the excess of liquor from the night before had given her a whopper of a headache.

How did she face Judson after her behavior the previous evening? Should she act like she didn't remember the whole wanton-in-the-kitchen episode? The unladylike begging for one itty-bitty kiss replayed in her mind. Among other things. *Ugh.*

"Good morning."

She groaned. Ready or not, time to face the music.

A deep chuckle rumbled in his chest. "Not feeling so well?"

She peeked through her splayed hands at the man who stood nearby. *Oh, thank the lord. He was fully dressed.* He leaned against the counter, the same worktop where her debauchery occurred the night before. Did he have no shame? Could he be oblivious to what had transpired the night before? Like all men? Clueless, every single one of them.

"Would you like for me to make you something to eat?"

He can cook? So, he'd set the tone. If he can ignore what had happened, then so could she. "Depends. Are you a better cook than Gramps?"

He laughed as he busied himself by filling a coffee cup. "Is he bad?"

"The worst."

Shifting, he retrieved the loaf of bread from the counter. "Walt showed me how to make toast the other day." He slid a glance in her direction. "I'm not sure you can handle anything heavier at the moment."

She nodded in agreement, and then moaned at the movement. "True." A cup of coffee appeared in front of her. She smiled at the nice gesture. "Thank you."

A few moments later he sat down at the table and placed a plate of toast between them. He sipped his coffee and caught her gaze. "Was I the reason you came home drunk last night? I mean, this week has been hard on you and my situation…well, is unusual."

She took a bite and chewed before she answered. "Believe it or not, no. Jess and I were having a nice time until Troy showed up. Again." She shrugged. "He'd been the last straw to a complicated week. I ordered a margarita and then another. Well, you know how the evening ended." She could feel a wave of heat make its way into her cheeks.

He lifted her chin with a finger. As their gazes collided he murmured, "I'm sorry."

Great. The best kiss she'd ever experienced in her life and he said sorry. She had crappy luck with men. Unless, hope blossomed, he didn't mean the lip lock. Dare she ask? "For?"

"Good morning. How is everyone this morning?"

She jumped in rueful embarrassment as she leaned away from his touch. "Morning, Gramps." Putting down her coffee cup, she stood. "I need to get ready for church."

She fled the kitchen as if hounds nipped at her heels.

"What's going on?"

Judson picked up his cup and took a sip before he met the other man's gaze. "Nothing."

He harrumphed. "I didn't stumble in on nothing, son. I could cut the tension with a knife. What have you done to my granddaughter?" He crossed his arms and waited for an answer.

He ran a hand over his face. "When Jess brought her home last night, Sadie'd had too much to drink."

"She was drunk?"

"Yes, sir."

He frowned. "That's not like her. What does her being inebriated have to do with the strain I sauntered in on?"

He splayed his hands. "I kissed her."

A grin appeared on the old man's face as he pumped a fist in the air. "Yes."

He stood and paced the floor. "I shouldn't have taken advantage of her while she was drunk." Another thought entered his head. He pointed a finger at him. "Why did you lead me to believe Jess was a man?"

A flash of what appeared to be guilt crossed Gramps' face for a brief moment before it disappeared. He shrugged. "I can't help you jumped to conclusions."

A snort escaped. Now he understood the full extent of what she had to put up with on a daily basis. He shook his head as he opened the back door. "I'll go and take care of the horses."

"We'll leave for church around ten."

He acknowledged Gramps' words with a nod before he stepped out onto the porch.

*****

She fidgeted as Judson's leg brushed against hers…again. Was his touch on purpose? Sneaking a glance from under her lashes, she observed his profile. His gaze was focused on the preacher, giving no indication or awareness of his movements.

She scooted closer to Jess on the pew. This attraction for the man by her side drove her crazy. She hoped no one wanted to discuss the details of the sermon today, because between the distraction and the slight headache she still suffered from, her focus was MIA.

Her friend elbowed her in the ribs and passed her a note. She glanced about before she unfolded the written missive. A snort emerged. Mrs. Travis in the pew behind shushed them. She turned and mouthed, "I'm sorry."

She twisted back around and poked Jess in the side. "Well?"

She read the note again. *He's hot. Seems so much nicer than Troy. Why fight it?* Why indeed? She'd never gotten around to telling her friend where their guest hailed from the night before. Was Gramps correct about the wormhole? If he was, her attraction didn't matter. He would be gone. Back to where he belonged.

She took the pencil from the holder in front of her and wrote *it's complicated* on the note and handed the note back.

Moments later the preacher dismissed the congregation and she spied a woman a couple of pews over casting a wary glance her way. She frowned. Tracy attended the same church? Why had she never noticed? The other woman stood and watched her as she wrung her hands.

She turned to Gramps and Judson. "I need to speak to someone. I'll only be a minute, if you want to wait outside." She gave her best friend a hug. "I'll call you later." As they strolled away she waved goodbye to Jess's husband, David.

Tracy tensed as she stopped in front of her. "Good morning. How are you?"

"Hello." She shrugged her shoulders. "I'm fine."

She smiled to put the other woman at ease. "I didn't realize we attended the same church."

"I don't usually. My cousin invited me to join her." Silence reigned a moment before she continued. "How's your grandfather?"

She chuckled. "He's bounced back. Not much keeps him down for long."

"Great news."

She titled her head. "Tracy, about Troy."

The other woman tensed. "What about him?"

She spied the ring still in place on her hand. The lying beggar. Did the couple even argue and fight the other night? "I'm not in love with him. Sure, my feelings were hurt when I first found out what happened, but over the last couple of days I realized my heart hadn't been engaged." She extended her hand; "I'm happy for you and wish you all the happiness you deserve." Should she tell her how he'd acted over the last few days?

"Thank you."

She chewed on her lower lip. "Can I caution you, though? Ask him what he's been up to the last few nights."

Tracy frowned as a confused expression crossed

her features. "Why do I need to ask him where he's been?"

She placed a hand on the other woman's arm. "Because he was out at the farm Friday night and told me you'd broken your engagement, but I see you still wear his ring. You seem like a nice lady and I don't want to see you hurt."

She twisted the ring on her finger as her eyes misted. "He's been off since we ran into you at the mall. I hoped his sulking would pass, but he was at my house last night moodier than before."

A flash of guilt washed over her as she realized she might be the reason for his bad attitude. "That may be my fault. He confronted me while I ate out with a friend last night. I told him there couldn't be a relationship between us. I'm afraid I dented his ego."

Tracy tilted her chin and clenched her jaw. "I feel it's past time to have a heart-to-heart talk with my fiancé."

Sadie grinned as the other woman stalked from the church. Should she feel sorry for Troy? Not a single thread of regret wove through her body. She shook her head. He deserved to be berated.

Emerging into the sunshine, she paused on the steps. Gramps, Judson and Rita stood in a semi-circle laughing at whatever story Gramps told. She studied Judson a moment, unobserved. He seemed relaxed. Yesterday's tenseness not evident in his body language. The deep rumble of his laugh drifted across the church lawn. It was too bad he hadn't much to be amused about over the last few years. He had a wonderful laugh.

The threesome didn't hear her approach. "What tall

tales is he spouting now?"

Rita laughed. "Good morning, Sadie. When isn't he telling some kind of story?"

She witnessed a blush stain her grandfather's cheeks. The old smoothie must like Miss Rita more than he let on. And if the sly peek she threw his way were any indication, the feeling was mutual. "Rita, could I ask a favor?"

"Sure. What do you need?"

Sadie patted Gramps on his shoulder. "Could you make sure this guy gets home?"

He frowned. "You're not taking me?"

"I thought I would take Judson into Kansas City for a day of relaxation and fun." Her gaze locked upon his. "I think it's what the doctor ordered."

"Walt, would you like to join me for lunch? Afterward I can take you home?"

He locked his elbow through Rita's. "I'd be delighted." Over his shoulder he called, "You young'uns have fun."

Chapter Twenty-Four

She shot a quick glance at her quiet passenger. He hadn't said much since they'd left the church. "So, Judson." She waited until his gaze met her own. "Care to tell me where you're from?"

His lips quirked. "Haven't I said?"

She bit her lip as she played their conversations over the last few days in her mind. Taking one hand off the steering wheel, she shook a finger. "Uh-uh. You dodged the question. I'm not letting you get away with not answering this time."

He chuckled and shrugged his shoulders. "What do you want to know?"

"A good place to start would be where you're from." She flung another accusing finger in his direction. "Don't you dare say Kansas. I know that much already."

He held up his hands in mock surrender. "I'm not sure where I grew up exists in your time. Ever hear of Black Jack, Kansas?"

She frowned. "I'm not sure I have."

"The town got its name from a nearby creek. It was also a supply stop along the Santa Fe Trail."

"Hey, pretty cool."

"My family's farm was about half a mile outside of Black Jack and Baldwin City was a couple of miles away."

She tilted her head. "Wait. Baldwin City isn't far from our farm." A chuckle emerged. "You're a local boy." *Man*, her mind corrected. "Well, over one hundred years ago anyway."

A soft chuckle escaped from his lips. "I guess I am."

"What else can you tell me?"

A moment of silence passed before he asked, "Ever hear of a man named John Brown?"

Why did the name sound familiar? Brown, a common name. Unless…she gasped. "The abolitionist? That John Brown?"

He shrugged. "I guess. He led an attack on Black Jack in the year eighteen fifty-six" Amazement rattled her brain. A distant memory of Kansas's history sparked in her mind. He referred to the Battle of Black Jack. Why hadn't she recalled the name before when he'd told her about his family's farm? The encounter may be the first armed conflict between proslavery and antislavery in the United States. An unexpected sadness eroded her body and clogged her throat. He'd experienced a harder life than she could imagine. And he wanted to risk going back. Duty bound by orders given a soldier.

She swallowed the lump in her throat. "Well, today you and I will have some fun. I think you deserve a little entertainment before…well, before you know." The words "go back" were left unspoken between them.

A strange expression passed over his features before his mouth quirked at one corner. "What did you have in mind?"

Had his voice lowered? Neither had brought up the steamy kiss from the night before. Was it possible he relived the lip lock as well? She shook her head to dispel the image. A nervous laugh escaped. "Nothing illegal…or indecent." Her gaze met his. No doubt about it, his smoldering stare said he remembered and he wouldn't mind indecent.

She cleared her throat. "We're almost there. I'm taking you to the Legends shopping area in Kansas City. They have food, fun and shopping. We'll start with lunch." He didn't reply right away. She glanced over to see him frown. "You're not hungry?"

He shook his head. "No. Hunger isn't the problem. I've enjoyed so many new foods while I've been here, I'm not sure what to ask for."

She chuckled. "No worries. We'll go somewhere with many food choices and the options will blow your hundred-year-old mind."

He leaned across the truck's seat and brushed her cheek. "I've no complaints about your cooking. You and Walt have taken good care of me. I can't thank you enough."

His touch set off thousands of butterflies fluttering within her stomach. Why this man? His leaving would hurt worse than Troy's betrayal and she didn't want to wrap her head around why. Not at this time. She forced a smile to her lips. "You're welcome." She forced her gaze back to the front and looked for a spot to park.

He studied her profile as she concentrated on parking the truck. Did she have tears in her eyes? For him? He swallowed and looked out the side window. The idea of leaving became harder each day.

"We're here."

Startled from his reverie, he glanced about. The advancements in this day and age still amazed him.

Metal beasts were everywhere. More than he'd seen up to this point. People milled about in front of a line of large buildings.

She dropped the keys into her purse. "Ready for some great food and entertainment?"

He opened the door. "Lead the way."

Moments later he stopped suddenly, his mouth agape. Inside the doorway they'd entered, unidentified noises and lights filled the room.

She giggled to his left. "Ready to have some fun?"

Once settled at a table with a menu in front of him, he asked, "What is this place?"

She smiled and waved a hand. "This, my friend, is a kid's playground for adults."

A young man stopped by their table. "Good afternoon. My name is Randy and I'll be your server. Can I get you a drink or an appetizer?"

"Hi, Randy. We'll start with a couple of waters while we peruse the menu."

Judson glanced at the thick paper in his hands. Pictures of drinks and food were displayed on each page. So many choices. How did one make up their mind?

"Would you like to try a beer?"

His mouth watered. When had he last had a beer? "Yes. How about you? Will you have one?"

She shook her head and grimaced. "Oh no. I'm still recovering from the alcohol I consumed last night. Today it's all you."

Chapter Twenty-Five

Hours later she lay on her bed, her hands behind her head. She smiled as she recalled the events from the afternoon. He'd enjoyed the activities like a little kid in a candy store. Watching him learn and play games would remain a priceless memory she'd cherish.

She chuckled as she remembered him shooting hoops and calling out, "He shoots, he scores," when the ball swished through the net. Words he'd picked up from her.

After the restaurant they'd enjoyed a matinee movie. She snuggled deeper into her pillow. A most pleasant afternoon.

Her smile disappeared as an unexpected pain bounded up her spine. If he left how would she handle herself? He wasn't leaving for a day or so, but for the rest of her life. How had he wormed his way into her heart in such a short period of time? A wave of melancholy descended. Could she pinpoint what she felt? Lust? Pure and simple. Right?

His kiss from the previous evening invaded her thoughts. What if she never felt this way again? Could she let him disappear without tasting his lips one more time?

She leaned up on her elbows and glanced under her door to see a light ablaze down the hall. Was Judson up or Gramps? She nibbled on her lip. Should she contemplate approaching him for a goodbye kiss?

She flung her legs over the edge of the bed, then swung them back and flopped down on the mattress. *Girl, don't be stupid. Why did her conscience decide to show up now?* She silenced her thoughts and climbed out of bed.

Tiptoeing to the door, she opened it. The light she'd spied filtered from under the bathroom door.

A snore echoed down the hallway. Gramps. She smiled as her ears received the answer to her question. Judson occupied the bathroom. Neither spoke of what happened in the kitchen the night before the entire day. Would he even welcome the idea of a kiss? She leaned against the adjacent wall and nibbled on a fingernail. Suddenly she leaned up, her back snapped to attention. She didn't want just a kiss. Her body hummed in strange anticipation. She could hear the shower still running. Dare she be so bold? What would he think of her? Did she care?

An opportunity like this didn't come along often. She took a step forward and tried the door. Unlocked. Was she insane? Before she could change her mind, she opened the door and snuck in. Steam hovered in the room, covering everything like a blanket.

He hadn't heard her enter. He leaned against the shower wall, arms extended, and head bowed as the water pounded his back. A confidence she didn't know she had overtook her as she dragged her T-shirt off and shimmied out of her panties.

The click of the shower door reverberated in the silence as she entered the stall. His head reared back and his nostrils flared as his gaze locked onto her own. "Sadie."

"Shh." If they talked, she'd run from the room embarrassed about her bold advancements. She trailed a hand down his slickened chest following one of the water trails. His skin wasn't as pale since he'd spent a few hours outdoors over the last few days. But she could still make out scars marring his chiseled chest.

She let her gaze travel higher before she leaned up to place a tentative kiss on his lips, his unyielding beneath her own. Tears misted her eyes at his nonresponse. She'd misread his interest. The reason for her insanity wasn't alcohol this time. She should have known better. Taking a step back, she spun to let herself out of the shower before she made a bigger fool of herself.

A gentle hand upon her lower back stilled her escape. "Sadie." A guttural groan sounded behind her. "You make it hard for me to act a gentleman."

His words were soft, and she strained to hear them. Once she understood what he had said, hope surged through her veins. As he traced a path down her spine heat pooled in her body's core. She twisted, and their gazes locked. His was ablaze with an intense desire. So, she hadn't imagined the attraction. He tried not to act upon his desire. She leaned in close and whispered, "Maybe I don't want you to be a gentleman."

Another groan emerged as he ran a trembling hand through his wet hair. "You don't know what you're asking of me. What about Walt?"

She laughed and met his gaze. "You want to make this a threesome?"

An astonished expression passed across his features as he started to sputter. "Hell, no."

She giggled harder, dispelling some of her

nervousness.

"He'll kill me for taking advantage of his granddaughter."

She splayed her hands up and down indicating her body. "Do I, or do I not, come across as a consenting adult?"

He didn't answer as he studied her body, his gaze unflinching.

Confidence returned as she stepped closer and grasped the nearby bar of soap. "I think you've missed a spot of dirt."

His eyes closed, and his Adam's apple bobbed as she started to lather his body. As soon as she rinsed the soap, she leaned in and nibbled a trail from his neck to chest. His skin hot beneath her lips.

She gasped as he twirled her, as he took control and restrained her against the shower wall. The cool tiles not unpleasant on her fevered skin. The moan escaped her lips as he nipped along her neck. His touch was gentle yet demanding at the same time. Embarrassment and all thought dispersed as his hands magically brought her body alive.

Her eyes flickered open as coolness invaded her senses. Where had his body heat gone?

His passionate gaze studied her with an attentiveness that robbed her breath. His hand shook as he caressed her breast. "You're beautiful."

Her nipple puckered in response. She'd never felt as attractive as she did at this moment. The ache her body felt at his simple touch had her dazed. She'd never experienced the liquid heat thrumming through her body. Her hesitation deserted her as she ran a finger down his chest and farther to his erection. A powerful shiver raced through his body. They both seemed attuned to the same desire. "You're not too shabby yourself."

He leaned his forehead against hers. "I'm not sure I want to stop."

She turned off the shower before she took both of his hands. "I didn't ask you to."

Exiting the stall, she grabbed the nearby towel off the rack. A gasp escaped as he wrapped an arm around her waist and tugged until she was flush against his chest. The water droplets on their skin enhanced the sensual heat emitting from their bodies. The towel dropped to the floor as he nibbled on her neck. His hands moved from around her waist downward to the heat pooled between her legs.

Her. Body. Was. On. Fire. Holy crap. Shaking, she turned. "Your room. Now."

A smile quirked his lips as he whispered, "He shoots, he scores."

She laughed and tried not to trip over the discarded towels. "Gotta love a fast learner."

Did the opening of the bathroom door sound louder in the quiet house than normal? She couldn't believe she was sneaking around, naked, with a bare man close behind. His door stood ajar and she dashed across the hallway into the safe confines of his room.

The bedside lamp cast a soft glow about the room. A warm hand caressed her bottom, rekindling the urgency within her body. Too late she realized her plan hadn't included protection. Crap on a stick. He wouldn't be as prepared as a boy scout. She dropped her chin to her chest.

His deep voice pierced her disappointment.

"Sadie?"

She turned and noticed his frown of confusion. "I didn't think this through. I don't have any protection."

His frown deepened.

Did they have condoms in eighteen sixty-three? "I'm so sorry. But the last thing I need to happen tonight is to become pregnant."

He slipped out of their embrace and sauntered over to the nightstand. He opened the drawer and removed a bag from its depths. She followed, curious. Had her meddling grandfather placed condoms in the guest room? He withdrew a box from the sack.

"I saw Walt put this in the drawer the other day. When I asked him what they were, he shrugged and said something about insurance." His gaze met her own. "Is this what you need?"

Freakin' A. Her interfering Gramps had struck again. He needed to be reprimanded, but she'd address the matter later. Much. Later. Her hand shook as she took the box from his hands and tossed the container on the bed. "Where were we?"

Her breath escaped in a rush as he eased her down upon the bed. Her gaze met his. She witnessed a shadow lurking in his gaze. Not providing him a chance to think or change his mind, she peppered kisses up his neck and nipped at his jaw. She placed a hand against his chest. His heart rate increased under her fingertips.

"Sadie. Are you sure?"

She nibbled on her bottom lip before she nodded. At the moment she couldn't be any more positive and she wouldn't try to concern herself about tomorrow. When he disappeared from her life.

He captured her lips and eased down until the light

dusting of his chest hair rubbed her naked breasts. A gasp escaped. Her nerve endings danced as his uncertainty disappeared and his lips devoured first her neck, then her breasts.

She closed her eyes as her thoughts shattered and the flames from earlier surged through her veins. He rolled, and she found herself straddling his slim hips. His throbbing manhood pressed against her intimately. She smiled and stretched until her breasts once again brushed his naked chest.

"Are you trying to kill me?" His voice came out low and raspy.

She laughed but stopped as she found herself flipped and pinned beneath his body. She squirmed as he placed a kiss to her stomach before gracing first one thigh with a caress from his lips, then the other. "I can ask you the same," she croaked.

A husky chuckle escaped his lips. She fisted her hands in the sheets as his hot breath stroked her heated core. He eased up and settled between her legs. He studied her face a moment before he placed a gentle kiss upon her lips.

Multitasking had never seemed so challenging. Not breaking the contact, she grasped the nearby box and struggled a moment with the condom. Her gaze met his as she crossed her legs behind his waist and joined their bodies. Oh lordy. She'd thought his kiss was lethal. She'd never scoff at the romantics who expected fireworks. Ever again. Hold out for the explosives.

She whimpered as an intense pleasure overtook her. They cried out in unison as they exploded into a million pieces moments later. Liquid pleasure pulsed through her as her breathing returned to normal.

He rolled to the side and tucked her in close. "Sadie?"

She placed a hand to his lips. "Shh. No regrets. Not on my end anyway."

What had he done? He drew circles on her arm as he listened to her sigh in her sleep. He took a moment to relive, in detail, what happened. Making love to her hands down the most incredible thing he'd ever experienced in his life.

She'd said no regrets. What he'd done still didn't keep him from feeling like a scoundrel. He turned his head and placed a kiss upon her forehead. The fragrance from her hair wafted to his nose.

He closed his eyes and memorized the scent. For when he was back in his own time, he wanted to take all the memories he could with him. He didn't have any other choice. He had to try to go back. Didn't he? What type of soldier would he be if he neglected his duty?

He opened his eyes and let his gaze settle on her. The glow from the lamp danced upon her naked form. She nestled against his side. Something twisted inside his chest. He'd only begun to explore the attraction he had for her. No one ever said life would be fair. He should know, better than some. He shifted and leaned up on his elbow. She sighed and snuggled closer. He smiled as he studied her while she slept. Why shouldn't he enjoy the pleasures she had offered?

Shaking guilt from his mind, he leaned over and trailed his lips over the gentle curve of her neck. She smiled in satisfaction, stretched and brought their bodies closer together.

Her breath hitched as he sucked at a breast, before he nipped at its bud. His gaze met her sleepy one as he trailed down her stomach.

A husky laugh escaped her lips. "I've created a monster."

****

He consulted the clock on the wall. Pre-dawn. He realized he wouldn't sleep anyway as he eased his body away from her warmth. Days before his failed mission represented his biggest disappointment in his life. Now, he had a greater regret. Leaving the love he'd found made the previous failure pale in comparison.

He donned the now clean uniform he'd arrived in. He turned before he exited the bedroom to give her one last glance. Sorrow settled in his heart and he didn't think he'd shake the feeling any time soon.

Chapter Twenty-Six

"Don't stare at me with those accusing eyes. I know I'm guilty enough without you adding to my shame." Judson studied Sinatra's soulful gaze as the mini blinked in innocence. He scratched under the horse's chin. "I know, buddy. Sadie isn't the only one I'll miss."

A chuckle brought his conversation to an end. Walt stood inside the barn scratching his whiskered chin. "They have a way of creeping into your heart, don't they?"

Not just the horses, his mind screamed. "I couldn't sleep."

A knowing smile spread across the older man's face. Judson had never blushed before in his life but felt his cheeks heat now. The other man knew how he'd spent the last couple of hours. Would he make him go pick a switch like his pa used to whenever he'd gotten into mischief?

He cleared his throat. "Walt."

Walt held up a hand and stopped him mid-speech. "Been there, son. Don't make this anymore awkward."

He nodded, swallowed hard and asked, "Is it time?"

As they travelled the deserted dirt road, the stars twinkled down as if laughing at the mess he'd made of his life. His thoughts revisited the vision he had left in the warm bed back at the Winters' farm. If he did go back to where he belonged…he would forever miss her. His angel. Why did life have to be so complicated?

He shook off his wondering thoughts. "Do you have any idea what to search for?"

Walt didn't answer right away. "No. I figured we would know when we saw it."

Silence filled the truck cab as both retreated into their own thoughts. They hadn't travelled much farther when he noticed a slight haze in the field to his left. He pointed. "Walt. Look. That isn't normal. Is it?"

He pulled over and placed the truck in park. His heavy sigh echoed in the truck. "The sight is peculiar. I've never seen anything like it before in my life."

A shiver of anticipation, or dread, eased down Judson's spine as he got out of the truck. Dust danced in front of the truck's lights as he crossed to the side of the road. He stared in wonder at the wavy object just a short distance away. The image reminded him of heat rising above the earth on a hot Kansas day.

He turned to Walt. "If this works, I can't thank you enough for all you and Sadie did for me."

The older man cleared his throat. "Son, I know you have a sense of duty to the cavalry, but I'm asking you to stay. Not for my sake, but for Sadie's."

"I would if I could. I can't ignore my obligations I had before I met her. If there is a chance for me to change what happened in Lawrence, I need to take that chance."

"I understand, son. I don't like the idea, but I realize you have to see your orders through."

Judson stuck out his hand. "Wish me luck."

Walt surprised him as he tugged him in for a quick

hug instead of shaking his hand. "Take care of yourself and watch your six."

"Will do." He turned and approached the haze. A strange energy overtook him as he moved closer. The hair on his arms stood at attention. Anticipation shimmied down his spine. He took a quick glance back to where Walt waited before he entered into the vapor.

Chapter Twenty-Seven

Her eyes flew open. A wave of dread travelled down her spine. Deep in her bones down to the bottom of her feet. She knew. He was gone.

A sob rose in her throat as a sharp pain made its way through her chest. Her body hummed from the recent lovemaking, but her mind remained numb. She'd told him she'd have no regrets. But she did. Not the fact they'd made love, but they wouldn't be together.

A tear slid down her cheek as she gazed at the vacant pillow beside her, the indention his head made still visible in the dim light. At the top of the pillow sat a small wooden horse. The carving he'd worked on over the last few days. Indeed, he'd captured the likeness of her miniature horses.

She rose from the bed and glanced around for something to wear. One of his discarded shirts lay on top of the dresser. Of course, the polo had to be the one matching his eyes. She wiped the tears from her face before dragging the shirt over her head. She inhaled. His scent still lingered on the fabric.

Opening the bedroom door, she peeked down the hall. All she needed to add to her heartbreak would be for Gramps to witness her walk of shame back to her room. She scurried down the hall unnoticed.

****

Why had she come to work? Her focus sucked. She

sat at her desk and stared out the window, not seeing the activities going on outside. She hadn't seen Gramps before she left the house. And worse yet she hadn't heard from him.

A foreboding had flooded her body when she awoke this morning. She knew deep down they'd been successful. She'd been upset to find they'd snuck out without her in the middle of the night, but she understood. Accompanying him would put a strain on her already raw heart.

With a glance down, she rolled the small miniature horse in her hand. The wood warmed at her touch. The piece was beautiful. He had a gift. He'd made the piece of wood come to life.

Tears pricked her eyes. She blinked them away before they fell. Troy's deception paled in comparison to the loss she felt this morning. No matter how much she rubbed at her upper chest the burning sensation wouldn't cease.

"Are you all right?"

Startled she wiped at the escaping tears from her cheek before looking at her co-worker who stood in the doorway. Should she lie? Proof she wasn't okay lay wet on her cheeks. "No, Ann. I'm not."

"Want to tell me what has upset you?"

She attempted a shrug. "I'm not sure talking would help."

"Please tell me the crying rampage wasn't brought on by your ex."

"Troy? Good heavens, no."

"I'm glad. He wasn't the one for you."

A fresh set of tears formed. Ann hit the nail right on the head. The right man had come along and he was gone. Forever.

"Well, whatever you are upset over, Walt is in the lobby and his appearance isn't much better."

She rose and rushed to the reception area. Why hadn't Ann told her right away? His back and shoulders were tense as he faced outside as he stared out the lobby window. "Gramps?"

As he turned she noticed his blood shot eyes. He'd been crying. Hard. The only times she'd seen him cry were at her mom and grandmother's funerals. Sheer terror skittered down her spine.

His voice cracked as he asked, "Can we go to your office?"

She shut the door and leaned hard against the wood for support. Closing her eyes she prayed for strength, "What happened?"

He cleared his throat a few times before he found his voice. "It worked."

She frowned. She'd already had a premonition they'd been successful. What else had he expected? His distress worried her. "The news is awesome, right? It's what he wanted."

He nodded as his lower lip started to quiver. "I came to love the young man. I know you fought it, but you were in love with him as well."

Fresh tears pooled in her eyes as she acknowledged the truth. She'd been in love. True love this time and she'd let it slip through her hands. "Well, he's back where he belongs."

He leaned toward her desk and took a tissue from the box. He took a moment to blow his nose. "That's it. He is. But he isn't."

A shiver of trepidation wracked her body. "What

aren't you telling me Gramps?"

"Please sit down."

His request scared her further. She crossed the room and sat in her chair as she willed him to continue.

He took a deep breath. "I visited the Watkins Museum this morning."

Confusion and dread filled her mind. "Why?"

He shrugged his shoulders. "Curiosity. Pride. I don't know. I wanted him to succeed."

The tone of his voice changed. "But?"

He struggled for control before he continued, "Nothing had changed. Not one damn incident. Except one."

The blood drained from her face. An eerie foreboding travelled down her spine. She wasn't prepared for what he'd say.

His gaze met hers. "One more causality was listed that wasn't there before."

"No." She jerked in pain at his words. It wasn't …couldn't be true. She grabbed a tissue and dabbed at the unchecked tears.

He placed a hand to her shoulder. "I'm sorry, Sadie girl. I even had someone at the museum help me."

She picked up the wooden horse from her desktop. Images of Judson over the last few days inundated her mind. His vitality. Gone. Their lovemaking from the night before, more special now, more than ever.

A knock on her office door interrupted the horror of Gramps' words. Seconds later her boss stuck his head around the open door. "Oh, hi Walt, I didn't know you were here. Sadie, want to join us outside to observe the eclipse." He paused as he looked from Walt to Sadie. "Are you all right?"

Words failed her. She shook her head and didn't bother to try to stem the tears flowing down her cheeks.

"Do you need to go home?"

Emotion clogged her throat as she struggled to talk. "Cliff." She stopped and cleared her throat once more. "I'm sorry. Yes."

He studied her a moment. "Obviously something serious has affected you both or you wouldn't be in here behind closed doors bawling like babies." He turned to leave. "Please call me if you need my help. With anything."

She lifted her chin and forced herself to gain control. "Thank you, Cliff." She opened her desk drawer and retrieved her purse. Her gaze met Walt's. "You're taking me to where you left Judson. Now."

Chapter Twenty-Eight

With an owlish blink, Judson awoke. He lay prone on his back, the diminishing night sky spread out above. The last he remembered he'd stepped into a strange mist not far from the Winters' farm. Was he back? In his own time?

He eased into a sitting position. The acrid smell of smoke goaded his nose. Did someone nearby have a campfire? Or had his worst fear been realized? He'd made it back to eighteen sixty-three, but once again he was too late to warn Lawrence.

A wave of dizziness assaulted him as he sprang to his feet. He turned in a circle as he fought to get his bearings. Which way to town? Pausing in his panic, he closed his eyes and sent up a quick prayer for guidance.

The silence of the dawn splintered as a distant gunshot echoed across the meadow. He jerked to attention. What direction had the noise sounded? He stumbled as he spun and ran. A spasm clenched his stomach. A familiar fear ebbed throughout his body.

He shoved through the trees and dropped to his knees. Why? Was he destined for failure? Sadie and Walt had warned him. No matter how hard he tried, he wasn't fated to stop the raid on Lawrence. His heart broke as he stared at the smoke rising in the distance.

A sense of worthlessness washed through his body. He'd not changed a thing by coming back. He'd sacrificed so much. A growing love and a friendship with the Winters. The beginning of a new family. Not to replace the ones he had lost, but to move on and live.

"Looky who we have here, Earl. Mister, you must be like a cat. How many lives do you have left?"

The voices he'd prayed he would never hear again sent chills down his spine. He inhaled a sharp breath before he twisted to gaze into the eyes of the two men sitting upon their mounts. Les' tobacco stained lips upturned in a sneer.

"Seems we left a job unfinished, Earl. The boss won't be happy with loose ends." Les tilted his head and frowned. "For someone we shot last night you sure appear healthy."

He stood, braced his feet and straightened his shoulders. "Do what you must, Les. I don't want to be around to witness the carnage you played a part in."

Les spit a stream of tobacco, tossed his head back and laughed. "You're a brave one. I'll give you that. Yes, sir, no weakness from you."

He didn't answer. He'd passed helplessness ages ago. Les drew and cocked his pistol. He stiffened his resolve. "Don't make idle threats. Go ahead. You've wanted to put another bullet in my hide since you spotted me. I don't understand why you let me go the first time, considering the murderer you ride with."

"A mistake. One I'm going to mend right this minute."

He closed his eyes. Not in fear, but to visualize his sweet angel. His body jerked as the bullet ripped through his body.

****

She hadn't argued when Gramps had asked to

drive. She'd been too upset. The radio played low in the background. Neither spoke as each wrestled for control of their emotions.

A sob emerged as she recognized Chris Cagle's voice singing. The words to the song pierced her heart like an arrow hitting its target.

"Sadie, girl?"

She silenced the radio. "Don't. I can't..." Her voice broke on another sob.

Moments later she came to the realization he had parked. She wiped the stray tear from her cheek with her sleeve.

"This is where we saw a weird misty haze." He pointed to the left. "Over there."

She gazed at the spot he indicated. The lunar eclipse everyone observed cast an eerie gloom across the land. She opened the door and stepped out. She'd forgotten about the eclipse occurring this week.

Footsteps from behind had her tensing and she turned in expectation.

"I'm sorry, Sadie. It's just me." He put a supportive arm around her shoulders.

She leaned into him, gaining strength from his support. The last few days she'd gone from heartbroken over a man who'd been a zero to falling in love with a hero.

"I'm sorry, sweetheart."

She patted his hand. "I know, Gramps."

"Let's go home."

She shook her head. "In a bit. Give me a few more minutes."

A chill stole down her spine. The slight breeze played tricks on her ears. She swore she'd heard her name whispered on the wind. "Gramps, wait. Did you hear something?"

He tilted his head and listened. "No."

This morning's shock had her hearing things. As she turned, another strange noise carried on the hot afternoon breeze. She wasn't imagining the sound. Her gaze swung to a nearby grove of trees. Something wasn't right.

An eerie silence hung heavy in the air. Moments before birds had chattered gaily in the trees. "Listen."

He shifted over to where she stood. Seconds ticked by. "I don't hear anything."

"Exactly." Moving on pure instinct, she started toward the trees.

She studied the ground. What did she expect to find? She wasn't sure. As she broke through the foliage, she gasped.

Gramps stumbled into her from behind at her abrupt halt.

She stared in wonder as a haze floated above the prairie grass. Through the mist she glimpsed the town of Lawrence in the distance. Smoke spiraled from some of the buildings. "What are we witnessing, Gramps?"

He cleared his throat. "I don't think it's the current Lawrence, but the city of the past."

She blinked, but the vision didn't disappear. "Is the town real?"

"I believe so, but not for us on this day and time."

Her feet felt like lead as she took a tentative step forward.

He grabbed her arm from behind. "What are you doing? Don't go near that...thing. You don't know what it will do."

Of course he was right. What had she been thinking? They didn't understand the phenomenon in front of them. Judson had disappeared inside of the mass earlier this morning. And consider what befell him. He'd died.

She turned away from the sight of the smoke and destruction. "Gramps, let's go home." She'd taken a few steps when her grandfather's shaky voice stopped her.

"Oh my God."

She twisted about to see what had caused his distress. She glanced in the direction of his pointing finger. There inside the vapor to the right a lone figure lay prone in the prairie grass. A curse burst from her lips before she sprinted toward the shimmering image.

"Sadie girl, no. Stop."

She fought off her grandfather's firm grasp. "It's Judson, Gramps. I know it is. He's hurt or dying. We have to help him."

He shouted. "You can't go in there all willy nilly. I can't lose you too."

Tears streamed down her cheeks as she closed her eyes. "I can't stand here and watch him die. Not if I have a chance to save him."

He ran a shaking hand through his grey hair. "We need a plan. I don't want you to go in after him, get stuck and not be able to come back where you belong." He rubbed a hand down his face. His gaze met hers. "A rope. I have one in the back of the cab. I'll go get it."

She grabbed his arm. "Stay here. You have a bum ankle, I can get the rope faster." Her heart tripped inside her chest as she rushed the short distance back to the truck. She threw the items around on the floorboard. A wave of panic gripped her when she couldn't locate the twine right away. Maybe he'd been mistaken.

A surge of elation filled her as she found what she sought under the front passenger seat. Seconds later she burst through the trees and wanted to curse again. The mist wasn't as strong. Their time was running out.

"Quick. Tie the rope around my ankle. I'll go in and retrieve him." He shook his head. "No. I'm going. You can't stop me. I've got to try. Me. Not you."

Gramps' hand shook as he tied the rope. "Sadie." He swallowed hard. "Please, be careful. If things seem like they're going wrong, I'm yanking you out of there. Whether you have Judson in tow or not."

She inhaled a deep breath and let it out.

"Don't test me. You don't go if you can't promise to get out if you can't save him."

Seconds ticked by before she nodded. She didn't want to come back without him. She gritted her teeth and declared, "I'm ready."

A strange energy crackled as she neared the mist. She fought off a sudden wave of dizziness. Blocking the destruction of Lawrence from her mind, she focused on the still form. She didn't want to entertain the idea he was already dead. He couldn't be. Not when she'd found him.

She stretched a tentative hand through the vapor and found herself on the other side. The smell of smoke and death assaulted her senses. Each hung in the air as thick as a cloud.

She'd done it. She crossed over into the past. Eighteen sixty-three. A day in Kansas history she'd only read about up to this point.

A relieved sigh flowed from her as a faint moan

escaped his lips. She tugged on the rope as she stepped farther into the meadow. "Judson?"

Not a word or a single stir. She fought the rising panic in her body. Another step and she glanced back. Gramps stood on the other side worry etched upon his face. A few steps more. Her knees buckled as she dropped by his side.

A bright red stain tainted the front of his shirt. She unbuttoned his top to examine the damage. Her fingers shook in her haste. She gasped as blood oozed from a bullet wound in his abdomen. She swallowed her terror as she ripped a strip of cloth from his shirt to put pressure on the wound. Her other hand shook as she felt for a pulse at his throat. A faint heartbeat thrummed against her fingertips. A shaky sigh escaped. He was alive, but for how long?

"Judson? Can you hear me?" His pallor worried her. She hadn't thought how she'd get him back through the hole. You were never supposed to move an injured person, but she had no choice. With determination she rose, grabbed his ankles and struggled to drag his body.

She bit her lip. He hadn't uttered a sound. The jarring hadn't brought him back to consciousness. Was she too late?

Sweat broke across her brow. Determination filled her. She stood and glanced at the last few feet. The mist had dimmed over the last few minutes. She couldn't leave him here to die. A murmured prayer sprung from her lips as she prayed for the Lord to give her strength.

Gramps gestured with wild gestures from the other side as he shouted words she couldn't hear. He started to heave in haste at the rope.

Stay on target. She leaned down and grappled with his hand, sliding him around. In slow motions she backed up. Moments later she struggled through the hole, but his hand and shoulder were all that protruded from the haze. "Gramps, quick. The wormhole is about to disappear. Help me drag him the rest of the way before this blasted thing closes."

"Dag nab it, I told you. Didn't you hear me?"

She swiped at a trail of sweat pooling on her forehead. Her limbs trembled with a mix of exertion and adrenaline. "I need help. I can't haul him the rest of the way." A moment of panic set in as he stumbled on the uneven ground. She caught him before he fell. She glanced at the shimmering haze as it dimmed further before her gaze. "On the count of three, help me tug. One. Two. Three." She gripped him under his exposed arm and Walt grabbed his hand. They both heaved at the same time. The air crackled with a strange energy as the mist released Judson's unconscious body. They fell on their butts as the vapor and wormhole vanished before their eyes. A wave of disbelief travelled through her mind. The whole scene seemed like some sci-fi movie. But they'd done it. They had brought him back.

"Gramps, call nine-one-one." She crawled a short distance and leaned over his body. Her lips trembled as she tried not to cry. She speared her hands through his short locks. "Don't you dare die. I can't have another person I love leave me behind. Do you hear me?"

She wasn't sure what she'd expected. But when his gorgeous eyes didn't even flutter, she worried they'd gotten to him too late. Sirens sounded in the distance. Please, don't let them be too late.

"I'll meet the EMT's and lead them over."

Her teary gaze watched Walt rush through the grove of trees. Why? Why did life have to be so problematic?

A strangled cry escaped as an EMT rushed toward them. The police officer who'd been out to the farm only days before trailed along after them. A gunshot wound to the shoulder was one thing to explain, but one to the abdominal area…an altogether different story.

She eased away from him as they prepared to transport him to the hospital. "Can I ride with him?"

"I'm sorry, ma'am, but we don't have room."

She nodded and backed up a step.

"I'll drive you."

She met the gaze of Officer Williams and knew they had to come clean. No matter how farfetched the story. "Thank you, Officer."

Gramps placed a hand on her arm. "I'll meet you at the hospital. Everything will be all right. You'll see."

She dredged up a smile. Doubts plagued her mind, but she didn't verbalize them. She turned to follow the paramedics.

"Ms. Winters."

She stopped and glanced back at the officer. His gaze studied her feet. "I think you're forgetting something."

She peeked down and realized she still had the rope tied to her ankle. She dropped to a knee and made short work of untying the hindrance. "I'll try to explain in the car."

"I wish you would."

Chapter Twenty-Nine

"Stop your god-awful pacing. You're giving me a headache."

She jerked at Gramps' rough command. She'd forgotten he occupied the room. She splayed her hands and exclaimed, "I can't help it. Do you blame me? What is taking so damn long?"

He groaned. "Shhh. Quit cussing. You're in public."

Feeling chastised, she plopped down in a chair. "Sorry." There were days he could reduce her to an impertinent child with a few words.

He picked up where she left off, pacing the surgical lobby. "Sadie girl, you know surgery takes awhile and this type will take longer than a normal one."

She surged back to her feet. "I know, but we've been here for a couple of hours already."

He placed a calming hand upon her shoulder. "Honey, I know. But I have a feeling down deep in these old bones everything will be okay."

"He'd lost so much blood before…" she leaned in and whispered, "well, you know, when we hauled him back to the present." Listen to her spouting about time travel and wormholes. A few days ago those subjects were pure malarkey in her mind. Today had proven her wrong. On so many levels.

She cared about the man in surgery struggling to

survive. For days she'd denied her feelings as they flourished. But today when she found him lying shot and left for dead, she'd realized how much her affection had grown. In a few days. Her relationship with Troy proved to be a measly crush compared to the love she felt for Judson.

She stared at the double doors that led back to the operating rooms. She prayed she hadn't waited too long to tell him how she felt.

"Sadie?" Walt cleared his throat and waited until her gaze met his. "You haven't uttered a word and I'm dying to know. Your ride with the police…" He leaned in close. "How did you explain the shooting to Officer Williams?"

She put her hands to her temples, gently massaged them before she groaned. His worry was justified, and she couldn't believe he'd waited this long to ask about the officer. She sighed. "I told him the truth. Every single detail from the beginning."

He opened his mouth, closed it, and opened it again.

She giggled. "You look like a fish."

He found his voice after a few seconds. "This isn't a laughing matter."

Her merriment died in her throat. "Don't you think I realize that?"

"You even told him I lied."

She nodded in affirmation. "Yes, Gramps. All. Of. It. I came clean."

He croaked. "What will happen?"

She shrugged her shoulders and asked, "Before or after he sends the men in the little white suits for me?" She had no idea how the situation would play out with the police. The officer had listened to her story, stared straight ahead and hadn't uttered a word. His silence unnerved her in the tight confinement of the patrol car. As he'd arrived at the hospital his gaze met hers. She'd asked him if he believed her. The only words he murmured were, *I'll be in touch.*

Gramps' curse brought her back to the present. "I'm serious. Will I serve some jail time? Orange isn't my color."

She gaped at her grandfather. "You're seriously worried about what color looks good on you right now while Judson's fighting for his life?"

The big double doors opened as the doctor entered the waiting room. They waited for him to remove his mask. He appeared worn out.

"Are you Mr. Stone's family?"

Dread travelled down her spine. She'd not thought of the hurdle he'd presented. They weren't his true family. Could the doctor share information? Or would the new health care laws prohibit them from talking to the doctor?

Gramps cleared his throat. "We're not blood relation, but we're the family he has in these parts."

She waited with baited breath as the doctor eyed each of them before he nodded. A pent-up sigh escaped her lips.

"Mr. Stone had lost a lot of blood, but he's a lucky young man. I'm not sure the story would've been the same if he hadn't come in when he did. The surgery took longer because we wanted to make sure the bullet hadn't nicked any vital organs. He's resting comfortably in recovery."

She slumped in a nearby chair and struggled to

fight threatening tears. He was going to be okay. She swallowed hard at the thought of her arriving too late. The story's outcome wouldn't have ended happy. "When can we see him?"

"He will go to a room once he's out of recovery. Once he is situated he can have visitors."

She stood and shook the doctor's hand. "Thank you so much."

****

Exhaustion permeated her entire body. Her gaze blurred as she glanced at the blood pressure cuff expanding once again on his arm. Thirty minutes ago, the doctor had checked his vitals. Judson still remained unconscious with no improvement on his condition.

She laid her head on her arm resting on the bed and grasped his hand. She smoothed his calluses on his palm with a soft caress. He was such a hard working man, but one who'd held and touched her with such gentleness. "Judson, if you can hear me, please, I need you to wake up. I hadn't realized how much I need you."

"Sadie girl?"

She wiped a stray tear from her cheek before she gazed at Gramps. You would think she wouldn't have any tears left to cry. "How long have you been standing there?"

"Long enough."

"I've been sitting here having a pity party for myself. I didn't get the chance to tell him I love him."

He placed a calming hand upon her shoulder. "He's a fighter. I don't have a doubt in my mind he'll make it through."

Releasing his hand, she rose and paced beside the

bed. "What if he doesn't feel the same as I do? My heart couldn't take a rejection. Not from him."

"Sweetie, he isn't Troy. I saw through the bum's intentions the moment I met him."

True. He's not your ex, the two timing scum. She chuckled. "That's an understatement."

"Why don't you go home? You need to get some rest. I'll sit with him and call you if his condition changes."

She gave her head a shake. "Thanks, but no. I want to be here when he awakes."

Chapter Thirty

As awareness returned, Judson clawed through the fog to consciousness. The acrid smell of smoke didn't infiltrate his nose. Had the fires been extinguished? The pain he'd experienced in his abdomen had dulled to a throb. Had he not perished from Les' bullet?

A familiar smell invaded his senses. Did he imagine the soft fragrance he associated with Sadie's hair? He inhaled, reveling in the scent. He frowned as another odor assaulted his nose. One he'd smelled when first waking in the year Twenty Nineteen.

His arm felt heavy as he scratched his nose. A gasp had him pausing in his actions. Next his sweet angel's voice reached his ears.

"Judson? Can you hear me? Are you awake?"

He struggled to lift his heavy eyelids. "Sadie?" How could she be here? The last he recalled he lay dying in a meadow outside of Lawrence in the year Eighteen Sixty-three.

When he opened his eyes, the angel leaning over him blurred. But no doubt lingered in his mind. Sadie. He blinked as he focused on the woman leaning over him. "Are you really here?"

She laughed and choked at the same time. "Yes."

Confusion flooded his mind. "How?"

She wiped tears from her face. "We'll save the story for later. Right now, I'll get the doctor and let him know you are awake."

So tired. He couldn't keep his eyes open. "Okay." He relaxed and eased back into a haunted sleep.

****

When he next awoke his vision had cleared. She sat in a chair next to the bed, asleep at an awkward angle. A soft snore escaped her lips. How? How had he returned?

He touched her soft cheek. She felt real. He hadn't dreamed her.

She awoke with a start and grasped his hand.

"Sorry. I didn't mean to scare you."

She cupped his hand to her cheek. "I'm glad to see you awake."

He leaned his head back against the pillow. "You snore."

She snorted in agitation. "I do not."

A chuckle escaped, and he winced in pain. No doubt he was alive, the discomfort proved the point.

"It's good to see you awake, young man."

He opened his eyes to spy an older man he didn't recognize standing inside the doorway.

"I'm Doctor Taylor. How do you feel?"

He laid his head on the pillow. "Like I've been shot."

The doctor chuckled. "Understandable, since that's what happened. Can you recall the details?"

His mind skittered back to the two men on horseback. Les and Earl. They'd found him again. He closed his eyes as the memory of his second failure at Lawrence replayed in his mind. "I remember getting shot, but I can't recall how I got back here."

The doctor nodded. "You were unconscious when

you were brought in, hanging on by a thread. You've been unconscious for two days. Your body is well on the mend. We'll keep you in the hospital for a few days to make sure you don't have any setbacks or infection." The doctor patted his hand. "You get some rest and I'll be back in a few hours to check on you."

His gaze met her sparkling blue eyes once the doctor retreated. "I know he didn't know the answer, but you do. How did I get here? Not the hospital, but back in Twenty Nineteen?"

She smiled and jutted out her chin. "I brought you back."

"Why did you bother?" He hadn't meant to sound ungrateful, but the roughness of his voice caused her to flinch.

She stood and retreated a step. How could he have a happy ending to his life when so much unhappiness happened in Lawrence? He witnessed tears pooling in her eyes. How could he be such a bastard?

She turned and rushed out the door. "I'll leave you to rest."

Damn it, he didn't want her to leave. He needed her to help him assuage the guilt riddling throughout his body. "Sadie, wait."

The soft click of the door echoed through the silence in his hospital room. He leaned his head back against the pillow and begged the demons pounding in his head to diminish.

A sob escaped as soon as the door closed. She leaned against the wall and sank to her bottom. She stared at the adjacent wall. Numb with disbelief and pain. Why had she bothered to bring him back? His words ricocheted through her mind. The ungrateful man.

Had he wanted her to leave him to die? The intimacy they'd shared obviously meant more to her than to him. How could she have misunderstood? Again. She banged her head against the wall. Why did she always end up the fool?

"What are you blubbering about now? He's awake and doing well, ain't he?"

Great. Just what she needed. A reprimand from Gramps. She wiped a tear from her cheek and glanced up at her grumpy counterpart. "Why do you always show up when I'm falling apart?"

He smiled and shrugged a shoulder. "It's part of my job description."

She scoffed.

"My charming personality?"

She held up a hand. "Stop." She rose to her feet. "He doesn't want to be here."

He frowned. "What are you jabbering about?"

She paced a couple of steps. "Just now. After the doctor left the room, he asked me why I bothered to bring him back." She mocked, "I don't think the drugs were doing the talking."

He crossed his arms. "And? Did you tell the boy why?"

"Why do you insist on calling him a boy? We both know he's no such thing."

Unfolding his arms, he jabbed a finger in her direction. "Not the point. Did you tell him why?"

She paused. "Why what? What are you talking about?"

He harrumphed. "For such a smart young woman. Emphases on woman. You're being pretty dense."

"Hey." His words wounded her already damaged pride.

He muttered and shook his head. "Did you tell him you brought him back because you love him?"

She opened her mouth to reply and shut it again. Instant replay of the scene in her mind led her to the answer. No. She hadn't replied when he'd asked why but retreated from the room like a dog with its tail between its legs. Could the answer be so simple?

"That's what I thought. Such wasted foolishness. Get back in there and tell the boy you love him."

He was right, but she didn't want him to know. He'd get a big head. She smiled at the thought. Crossing to her grandfather, she kissed his wrinkled cheek. "I love you too." A blush blossomed and travelled up his cheeks.

He shoved her toward the door. "Go on, now."

She faced the door and squared her shoulders. She wasn't going down without a fight. This time she played for keeps.

The door flung open and banged against the wall. She cringed. Too much force. Cool your jets, she chastised herself. "You want to know why I brought you back, you ungrateful man?" She stopped mid-tirade when his haunted gaze collided with hers. His pain, mental and physical, contorted his features. The hurt he suffered wasn't because she'd dragged him back, but because of his damn mission. His lousy hero complex was lying exposed in front of her. "Oh Judson. It's not your fault."

He closed his eyes and shook his head. "Don't you understand? All those lives and destruction occurring that day was my fault. I had the chance to help. Twice."

She took his hand. "You can't change history. Don't you see?"

He entwined his fingers with hers. "No. I don't understand. I've tried."

Encouraged, she sat on the edge of the bed. "What happened in Lawrence had already occurred. It's been in our history books for years. You couldn't have changed what happened with the last fiber of your body."

He shifted. "But…"

"No. You're not a failure, Judson Levi Stone." She drew a hand from his heart to his head. "It's time for you to start believing not from here, but to this stubborn brain of yours."

He drew in a deep breath at her touch. "I'm not sure I can."

"You're not in this alone. Gramps and I will help." She smiled and leaned her forehead against his. "Even our four-legged motley crew is willing to help…if you'll let them."

He asked in a soft whisper, "What are you saying?"

She needed to take a leap of faith. She took a deep breath and released it. "Judson, you wanted to know why I brought you back." She leaned back to observe his nod. "I need you. Me. The stubborn independent woman who doesn't know when to ask for help."

Some of the shadows plaguing his gaze dispersed. "You need me?"

She swallowed hard and whispered, "I've fallen in love with you." She brushed her lips across his. "Although you weren't able to stop Quantrill's Raid… I couldn't stop you from raiding my heart."

He leaned up and took her face between his hands

and kissed her hard. "I love you too."

She met his urgent kiss head on as she tangled her fingers at his nape. A moan crept up her throat. Man, he could kiss. She gasped as she broke contact. "She shoots, she scores."

Chapter Thirty-One

Five months later

Judson stepped back to admire the piece of furniture that came to life by his hands. He caressed the wood and smiled. His friend, Brody Williams, would be happy with the piece.

Officer Williams had visited him in the hospital once he'd awakened. He'd been scared Williams would cart him off to jail. But to his surprise he'd helped him with a plan on how to explain his injury. Sadie's tearful confession on the ride to the hospital had touched a truthful cord within him. Once the formalities of the necessary reports were filed, they'd become fast friends.

He straightened and stared out the window. A dusting of snow had fallen overnight. The wind blew, and a chill made its way down his spine. He turned, popped open the wood burning stove and added a log.

The old potbelly glowed and flames licked at the new log. The stove purchase was a gift from Sadie. He'd needed the warmth since he spent so much time working in the shop. He glanced about the building with pride. The coins he'd carried in his pocket when he arrived sold for a pretty penny online. She amazed him with her ability to find information from her computer. She'd helped pick out the building design as well. Before too long his business took off. His projects were slow at first but the orders had poured in once word got out about his craftsmanship. The other night she jokingly said he was starting to earn his keep.

The mental and physical scars were almost gone these days. The Winters' love had helped with the healing. His conscience still bothered him, but the memories that haunted him were fewer and further in between. When she searched his name on the Internet after coming home from the hospital, the only information found was he'd been listed as missing in action and his body never located.

Since his business made him money, he planned to ask her to marry him. He'd gone into town today with Walt to pick out a ring. He'd given him his blessing, stating, "Son, it's about damn time."

Walt would be out with Miss Rita this evening. Tonight would be his opportunity to pop the question. His nerves hadn't quieted all day. She wasn't going to say no, or so he thought. But doubt sometimes plagued him.

A gust of wind swirled into the shop as she entered. "Brrr…I think Jack Frost bit my nose, moved down and took a bite of my butt."

He laughed and shook his head. God, how he loved her. "That cold, huh? I put another log on. Want to snuggle up with me?" He wiggled his brows.

She sidled up to him and wrapped her arms around his waist. "Now who in their right mind would turn down such a wonderful offer? Should I lock the door?"

He leaned down to nuzzle her neck. "There's no need. Walt isn't here."

She titled her head to give him better access.

"Mmm. I thought Brody planned on coming out today to check on your progress on his kitchen table."

He paused mid-nibble. "Crap, you're right. Do the thing with your phone and tell him not tonight."

She dragged her cell phone from her back pocket. "So, you want me to say, not tonight, honey, I have a headache?"

He chuckled as he unzipped her coat. He listened to her fingers as they flew over the keys of her phone. He unbuttoned her shirt.

"Damn. Would you stop. I need to concentrate or he's going to think he's getting lucky instead of you."

He removed his hands and held them up. "Can't have him thinking that, now can we?"

"Damn straight." A few seconds later she put the cell down. "Now, where were we?"

He smiled down into her upturned face. With a quick turn he pinned her body against the counter as he finished unbuttoning her top. Pink lace appeared. His lips captured hers as his hands spanned her ribs.

A shiver racked her body. He smiled against her lips before he lifted her onto the counter and aligned his body in the juncture of her legs.

"Wow. Someone is happy to see me." Her voice was husky with desire.

He chuckled, but stilled when he realized he'd left the ring box in his front pocket. So much for his big surprise. The fire crackled behind him as he stuck his hand in his pocket to retrieve the box.

Her blue eyes grew large and misted.

He opened the lid to reveal a small diamond surrounded by aquamarine stones. Walt had sworn she'd love the colored accents because they matched his eyes. Or some such nonsense. He hoped Walt hadn't led him astray.

She put a hand to her mouth and reached out with the other to touch the ring.

"I had planned a romantic evening, but I guess the cat's out of the bag. I love you. Would you do me the honor of becoming my wife?"

"Oh, hell yes."

He caught the ring box as she launched herself into his arms. "Such language, dear."

She leaned back with a sheepish smile upon her face. "Sorry. My answer is yes. If you hadn't gathered."

He lifted his hand to smooth a wisp of hair behind her ear. "I love you."

"I love you back. But you're taking too long. Can I actually wear the ring or is it only for display?"

Happiness bubbled inside his chest. He wiggled his brows. "I want to see you wearing the ring, but I want to see it against your bare skin."

She giggled and rid herself of her clothes.

Both smiled as he slipped the ring on her finger.

N. Jade Gray

Author's Note

The idea for Sadie and Judson's story was born from an article I read regarding the anniversary of the burning of Lawrence, Kansas by William Quantrill and his Raiders, occurring on August 21, 1863. With thoughts of a story churning in my head, I also experienced the total Solar Eclipse that occurred on August 21, 2017, a strange coincidence that seemed to fuel my imagination and add a mysterious twist to my story. Although the date needed to be changed to a current year for my story to fit our time period, I wanted to note the Eclipse really did occur on the anniversary of the raid one hundred and fifty-four years later.

I hope I fueled everyone's imagination on the "what ifs" that could occur during a natural phenomenon.

A word about the author...

N. Jade Gray grew up on a farm in Oklahoma with one sister and three brothers.

She began reading romance novels in high school and was hooked. In an attempt to entertain her friends, she began writing stories. The biggest hurdle she had to overcome with her writing was sharing her stories. Her former writing groups, the Wichita and Regional Authors and Low Country Romance Writers, helped with her confidence and shook the needed pom-poms to get her motivated for publication. She is also a former member of the Romance Writers of America.

She met her husband, Nathan, while attending college and has two grown sons, Blake and Mason. Not really knowing what she wanted to do when she grew up, she's held various jobs in the accounting and legal fields. She lives in Kansas with her husband, rescue cats Meera and Mango, and one spoiled dog named Fabio. Yes, she helped name the dog. She loves to hear her husband calling for his four-legged companion.

Thank you for purchasing
this publication of The Wild Rose Press, Inc.

For questions or more information
contact us at
info@thewildrosepress.com.

The Wild Rose Press, Inc.
www.thewildrosepress.com

To visit with authors of
The Wild Rose Press, Inc.
join our yahoo loop at
http://groups.yahoo.com/group/thewildrosepress/

www.ingramcontent.com/pod-product-compliance
Lightning Source LLC
Chambersburg PA
CBHW060052260626
47160CB00005B/1663